THE RUNAWAY DOLLS

DOLL HOUSES

26117. Solid wood. One of the most popular designs. Brick details. Facade with open door. Price.....$10.00

26118. High quality. Front opening doll house with brass hinges. Two chimneys. Eight rooms. Heart-shaped lock keeps dolls securely inside.

Price.....$13.00

26119. Shingled doll house with enclosed porch. Price.....$15.00

AUNT DOLLS

26120. Brilliantly decorated hat with pink bows. The costume is a work of art, made of the finest silk with lace trim. Ivory buttons. With bisque head and limbs, and painted hair. Price.$2.00

26121. Same: with violet coat and flowing hair.....$2.75

DOLL FURNITURE

26122. Made of hardwood with handsome carved back. This chair comes with oak table with turned legs. Price.....$1.00

KITCHEN SUPPLIES

26126. Tin kitchen set. Small size. Price.....$0.20

UNCLE DOLLS

26123. Bisque head. Tweed suit. Price.....$1.50

26124. Same as above with shiny gold watch chain. Price.....$1.75

26125. Same as above with striped suit and silk top hat. Price.....$1.85

DOLL SUNDRIES

26127. Doll hats. Assorted sizes. Price per pair....$0.10

26128. Doll booties. Crocheted in wool. Price per pair.....$0.1

26129. Embroidered silk doll coat. Each.....$0.40

We can't say enough about our

DOLL HOUSES ~

Best Goods. Low Prices.

BABY DOLLS
ASSORTED SIZES

26130. Full-jointed dolls. Finest bisque head. Long baby dress. Price.....$0.85

131. Superior quality ls with bisque head, wool ss. Price.....$0.75

26132. Fine lace dress with silk bow. Price.....$0.50

133. Large baby l. Full bonnet h lace trim. que head. ce.....$1.00

134. Fine h body, ple bonnet. ce.....$0.70

PAPA DOLLS

26135. Dressed doll with bisque head and limbs. Finest checkered suit. Height: four inches. Price.....$1.25

26136. Same as above with top hat and overcoat. Price.....$2.00

MAMA DOLLS

26137. Finest muslin and lace dress. Bisque head with painted hair. Smooth finish. Bisque hands and legs. Price.....$1.50

26138. Other mama dolls with various styles in dresses and hair. Price.....$1.50 each

GIRL DOLLS

26139. Our most popular doll. Fine pink ribbon and painted yellow hair. Full lace sleeves and undertrimmings. Price.....$1.00

26140. Same as above, but with pink party outfit and yellow toy balloon. Price....-$1.25

BOY DOLLS

26141. Bisque head and limbs with fashion-able sailor suit. Price.....$0.95

TINY BOOKS

26142. real bindings. Many titles. Set of ten. Price.....$0.75

Oliver Twist

Robinson Crusoe

---

close 2 order blanks in each Catalogue sent you, and will furnish more on application, free. It is not absolutely necessary to have these s, but they are a great convenience and prevent many mistakes. If you do not happen to have any handy, try to conform to the sample ng here given, to prevent error. PLEASE SEND ORDER BLANK TO US AT ADDRESS FOUND ON REVERSE.

(kindly cut along the dotted line)

SSRS. WILSON & SONS.
ican distributors of British goods
send to
e.
Office
nty.

How to be shipped (See rules in Catalogue, Page 1)
Enclosed please find $
The following items are selected from Catalogue No

No. of Article in Catalogue.	Quantity.	ARTICLES WANTED.	Sizes, Colors, etc.	Price.

Wilson and Sons
1 Scala Street
London, England

Willia
26 V
Reade

Seaborn Cox esq

...therby Lane

...onnecticut

America

ONE HU
YEARS

NDRED
LATER

The Mysterious Package

ANNABELLE DOLL didn't see the mysterious package when it was delivered. She didn't see it until late that night, in fact. Because Annabelle was a doll, and because she belonged to Kate Palmer, a tidy girl who always left the Dolls neatly posed in their Victorian house, Annabelle missed out on a lot of important things, and had to be content with hearing about them later.

Tiffany Funcraft was a doll too, but because she belonged to Kate's younger sister, Nora, who was careless and left things scattered everywhere, Tiffany happened to be wedged between two couch cushions (luckily with her head sticking out into the room) when the package was delivered, so she had a good view of the front door.

"What was mysterious about the package?" Annabelle wanted to know when Tiffany told her about it that evening.

"It was British," Tiffany replied.

Annabelle looked confused.

"I mean, it came from England."

"Well, that's not—" Annabelle started to say.

"It came from London," Tiffany rushed on, "but Mr. Palmer doesn't know anyone in London. I don't think Mrs. Palmer has seen the package yet," added Tiffany.

"Oh," said Annabelle.

"And it doesn't say 'Palmer' on the package. It's addressed to someone else."

"Well, then the package must not *be* for the Palmers," said Annabelle sensibly. She and Tiffany were sitting side by side on the floor of Kate Palmer's bedroom. The moon was full, and it shone through the window, making a pale square on the rug. Annabelle and Tiffany sat in the middle of the square, moonlight reflecting off Tiffany's body.

Annabelle sighed with pleasure. If there was anything better than a good mystery to solve, it was the freedom in which to solve it. And that was exactly what Annabelle and Tiffany had: two full weeks of freedom. Earlier that day, the Palmers had gone away on summer vacation, so ahead of the Dolls and the Funcrafts stretched fourteen glorious days without any humans around. Annabelle could scarcely believe her luck. The last time the Palmers had left for two weeks was before the Funcrafts had arrived, and before Annabelle had become quite so adventurous.

Annabelle looked down at her own body. It was made of china, and her hands and feet glinted in the moonlight (her face too, she supposed, although she couldn't see it). But she wasn't nearly as shiny as Tiffany, who was made entirely of plastic, including her snap-on clothing.

Annabelle's clothes, over a hundred years old, were made of delicate fabric and lace. Annabelle was fragile. She chipped easily, and her clothing was prone to ripping. Tiffany was sturdy and never had to worry about such things. But she was bound by the same rules as Annabelle and any living doll who had taken the oath and chosen to live by the Doll Code of Honor, the ancient principles protecting the secret life of dolls.

And this was why these two weeks were precious to Annabelle and Tiffany. As long as the Palmers were away, the dolls could roam about the humans' big house without putting dollkind in danger. They could sing and shout as loudly as they pleased. They could scramble up and down stairs. They could explore and laugh and play games. They could start projects (Annabelle wanted to learn how to knit, and Tiffany had found instructions for making a volcano) and finish them without worrying about what time the humans were due home. Annabelle hoped that her family, who lived in the old wooden dollhouse in Kate's room, and the Funcrafts, who lived in their new plastic house in Nora's room, could spend plenty of time together. She thought that the grown-ups in her family needed other adult doll friends.

"But the package *is* for the Palmers," said Tiffany. "At least, it's for somebody at this address. Twenty-six Wetherby Lane. I heard Mr. Palmer read that out loud. Then he said, 'This is our address all right, but not our name.'"

"That is strange," agreed Annabelle.

"Mr. Palmer is going to show the package to Grandma Katherine, but he'll have to wait until after they're all back from vacation. Grandma Katherine left yesterday for her trip, you know."

"Tell me again where Grandma Katherine went," said Annabelle, feeling slightly annoyed that Tiffany knew so much. Then she reminded herself that Tiffany had all this information because Nora was forever tossing her around the house and leaving her in uncomfortable places in which all Tiffany could do was stare vacantly and listen.

"Grandma Katherine is spending two weeks with her old college friends," said Tiffany. "In Massachusetts. Or Minnesota.

I'm not sure. And the Palmers are going to Monhegan Island."

Annabelle sighed. "The beach. I've never been to the beach."

"If somebody would just give Nora the Funcraft Travel Pack, number four eighty-one, we could have two beach chairs, a beach umbrella, a beach ball, a beach blanket, bathing suits, and sun hats," said Tiffany.

"That would be nice. But not the same as really going to the beach," said Annabelle. Her thoughts turned then to the fourteen days of freedom and all the things that could be done during that wonderful time. "Tiffany, let's go look at the package," she said. "Maybe we can solve the mystery. Where is the package? Do you know?"

"It's on the living room couch. Mr. Palmer put it there so he would remember to

show it to Grandma Katherine first thing after vacation. We can climb up the couch without too much trouble."

"All right," said Annabelle. "Just one thing—where's The Captain?"

"Closed into the back of the house. In the kitchen and the laundry room," replied Tiffany. "We don't have to worry about him."

"Good," said Annabelle, who had had many unfortunate experiences involving the Palmers' cat.

"Want to go right now?" asked Tiffany.

"Absolutely." Annabelle got to her feet. "I have to tell Mama and Papa we're leaving, though. Just a minute."

Annabelle hurried across the rug to the little stool, four steps high, under the Dolls' house. Kate was ten now and no longer needed the stool to reach any room in the three-story house that sat on a shelf several feet above the floor. But she had left the stool where it was, which was a good thing. Without it, the only way Annabelle could have gotten into or out of her house was in the hands of a human. Tiffany was lucky. The pink plastic Funcraft Dream House model 110 sat on the floor of Nora's messy bedroom. Tiffany could always run home in a jiffy.

Annabelle stood at the bottom of the stool and shouted, "Mama? Papa?" When there was no answer, she tried again more loudly. "Mama!! Papa!!"

"Yelling is fun, isn't it?" said Tiffany.

Mama Doll appeared at the front of the house, leaned over the edge, and looked down at Annabelle, which reminded Annabelle that one of the many small things for which she was grateful was that Kate hadn't closed and locked the front of the dollhouse before she'd left on her vacation. Kate had asked her mother whether she thought it would be a good idea, had even fingered the tiny key and the heart-shaped padlock, and peered into the Dolls' house in a way that made Annabelle wonder just how much Kate knew about their private lives. But in the end, Kate had left the house open, to Annabelle's immense relief.

"Annabelle? What on earth are you shouting about?" called Mama Doll.

And in that funny way that thoughts have of jumping into your mind from no place in particular, Annabelle was suddenly thrust back in time, more than a hundred years, to the day on which the old doll maker had completed Mama Doll and sat her on a wooden shelf in his workshop in London. Later, when the shop was quiet and the doll maker had gone home for the night, Annabelle had looked high above her at the doll who was to be her mama. Sitting in a row next to Mama had been Papa, Uncle Doll, and Nanny—who would become the children's nanny. Baby Betsy was sitting on another shelf since she was part of a different doll set, and Auntie Sarah and Bobby were not finished yet.

That night, another doll in the workshop, a living doll, had given Annabelle the oath, and she had dutifully repeated, "I, Annabelle, an avowed member of the race of dolls, do hereby promise to protect our secret life by upholding the Doll Code of Honor in accordance with its everlasting law."

The other doll had then explained that if Annabelle made a mistake or did something foolish, something to put the secret life of dolls in danger, she risked becoming an ordinary doll again. Being a living doll, a doll person, wasn't easy. But it wasn't boring, and Annabelle felt certain that being an ordinary lifeless doll must be quite boring indeed.

Tiffany nudged Annabelle now, just as Mama Doll said again, "Annabelle, did you want something?"

"Tiffany and I are going to go downstairs for a while, okay?"

For once, Mama Doll didn't reply with a list of warnings—warnings to be quiet, to be careful, to stay out of sight, and above all, to remember the consequences of foolish behavior. By this, she meant Doll State and worse, Permanent Doll State. Doll State, which Annabelle had had the misfortune to experience a number of times, rendered one motionless, nearly lifeless, for a period of twenty-four hours following an act that put the race of dolls in danger. There had been the night, for instance, long after the humans had gone to bed, when Annabelle, trying to escape from The Captain, had darted across a room and run into Mrs. Palmer's slippered foot. Mrs. Palmer had seen her and picked her up, troubled—and Annabelle had immediately found herself in Doll State.

She had been lucky, though: Twenty-four hours after Annabelle had gone into Doll State (after a whole day in which she had had nothing to do but think about her careless behavior), she had been released, and had received only a scolding from Nanny.

But there was always the threat of Permanent Doll State. Annabelle had seen only one doll—a horrifying visiting doll named Mean Mimi—thrust into what she thought was Permanent Doll State. This was Doll State that didn't end; it was twenty-four hours times eternity. A doll in PDS was thought to have committed an act so dangerous that he or she was a threat to the race of dolls, and therefore not to be trusted to continue as a living doll. Annabelle shuddered at the thought. How easy it would be to make a mistake that would result in PDS.

This, however, was not the time to worry about such things. Now Annabelle had her fourteen days of freedom. So she called thank you to her mother, and she and Tiffany ran from Kate's room and down the second floor hallway to the top of the staircase. As they scaled the steps—a process that used to take them much longer—Tiffany, puffing with the effort, said, "So what do you think the boys are going to do while the Palmers are away?"

"The boys" were Annabelle's brother, Bobby, and Tiffany's brother, Bailey. "I don't know," Annabelle replied. Then she added, "I think Bobby's keeping a secret from me."

"Me too! I mean, I think Bailey's keeping a secret from me," said Tiffany. "What do you suppose they're up to?"

"I have no idea. You know what my mother is up to, though, don't you?"

"Getting ready for the party?"

Annabelle nodded. "You know, she's never given a party like this before. Your family will be her first real guests."

"I wish our parents would spend more time together," said Tiffany, stopping herself before she added, "but your parents are too chicken to leave their house." She tried hard to put herself into the shoes of Mr. and Mrs. Doll, to remind herself that because they were fragile, and also, of course, from another era, they couldn't be as active and adventurous as Mom and Dad Funcraft.

Tiffany dropped down the last step, and a moment later Annabelle landed on the floor beside her. They ran to the living room.

"It's funny not to have to whisper, isn't it?" said Annabelle.

"Just think—we can be perfectly loud. LA, LA, LA, LA!" sang Tiffany. "OH, CAPTAIN, CAPTAIN, WHERE ARE YOU? WOULDN'T YOU LIKE A TASTY LITTLE DOLL MORSEL? WELL, COME ON AND GET US. OH, THAT'S RIGHT—YOU CAN'T! LA, LA, LA, LA!"

Annabelle, laughing, followed Tiffany into the living room, and the dolls climbed up the side of the couch.

"There it is," said Tiffany, pointing to a small package wrapped in brown paper.

The girls bounced their way along the cushions to the package. The writing on the label was hard to see with only the moon for light, but Annabelle read slowly, "'William Seaborn . . .'" She paused. "What's that last word?"

"It looks like '*Coxesq*,'" said Tiffany. "What kind of name is '*Coxesq*'?"

Annabelle peered at the name for a few more moments. "William Seaborn," she murmured. "Why does that sound familiar?" And then she raised her hand to her cheek.

"Tiffany!" she exclaimed. "His name isn't 'Coxesq.' It should say 'Cox *comma* esq.'—for *Esquire*. William Seaborn Cox, Esquire!"

"Who's William Seaborn Cox?" asked Tiffany.

"Well, I don't understand it at all, but William Seaborn Cox was the name of Grandma Katherine's grandfather, and he was the one who ordered our family and our house from the doll maker in London way back in eighteen ninety-eight. We were to be a gift for his daughter—Grandma Katherine's mother. So the doll maker packaged up Mama and Papa and Uncle Doll and Auntie Sarah and Nanny and Bobby and Baby Betsy and me, along with our house, and sent us across the ocean on a big ship."

"He sent the wrong baby, though, didn't he?" said Tiffany, who had heard this story before, but liked hearing it again.

"The *wrong* baby! No!" exclaimed Annabelle, picturing her giant baby sister. "He didn't send the *wrong* baby. He sent a baby from a much bigger doll set, but we love her, and she's the right baby for us. Anyway," she went on, "why has a package

been sent to William Seaborn Cox now?
He died nearly eighty years ago."

"I don't know," said Tiffany. "But your
family came from London, and Mr. Palmer
said this package came from London. Do you
suppose it's from the doll
maker?"

"Oh, it couldn't be.
He must have died
long ago too."
Annabelle squinted
at the package.
"Whoever
mailed this
has very
scrawly

handwriting.
It's so hard to read cursive.
I'm pretty sure it's from London, though."

Tiffany suddenly stood very still, her
hand at her ear. "Did you hear something?"
she asked.

"Like what?"

"Shh. There it is again. Listen!"

Annabelle frowned, concentrating, and after a moment she heard a little voice, not much louder than a bird chirp. "Hello?" it said.

"I did hear that!" exclaimed Annabelle. "Where did it come from?"

"Inside the box, I think." Tiffany kicked the corner of the package. Then she kicked it again.

"Hello? Who's there? Are you dolls?" said the teensy voice. "Can you hear me?"

Annabelle shrieked.

"Hello? Hello?" called the voice a bit more loudly.

"Tiffany, do you know what this reminds me of?" said Annabelle, awestruck.

"No. What?"

"It reminds me of when Uncle Doll and Bobby and I found *you*."

Annabelle remembered the night when she and her uncle and brother had been out searching for her lost Auntie Sarah and instead had come upon the Funcrafts, still boxed up with their Dream House, waiting to be presented to Nora for her birthday. Now Annabelle leaned over and examined the package closely. She saw a tiny rip in the paper, and she pressed her mouth to it. "Hello!" she called. "We can hear you! Who are you? My name is Annabelle. I'm here with my friend Tiffany."

"I'm Matilda May," said the tiny voice.

"What are you doing in there?" asked Tiffany.

"Don't know."

"You don't know why you're in a box?"

"No."

"Where are you from?" asked Annabelle.

After a long pause, Matilda May said, "Don't know."

"Don't you know *any*thing?" said Tiffany, exasperated.

"Tiffany, be nice," said Annabelle. She leaned toward the package again. "Matilda May, how old are you?"

"Um, one hundred?" guessed the voice.

"Are you a doll?" asked Annabelle.

"Yes."

"Then someone gave you the oath, is that right?"

"Don't know."

"Someone must have, since you can talk."

"Okay."

"How old are you in doll years?" Annabelle asked.

"Free, I fink," said Matilda May.

"Three?" said Tiffany.

There was a rustling inside the box, and Annabelle said, "Are you nodding your head?"

"Yes."

"Matilda May?" said Annabelle. "That's quite a long name. Could I call you Tilly May or just Tilly?"

"Okay."

"All right. Tilly?"

"Yes?"

"Where did you come from?"

"From the doll shop."

"A doll shop in London?"

"Don't know." A pause. "I fink so. I've been in this package a long, long time. One day a man picked up the package and said, 'Oh, my heavens, now how did this get here? Look how old it is.' Then he opened the package, then he sealed it up again, and then he mailed me. I was supposed to get mailed before, to Mr. Cox, but the box fell and no one found me."

A funny feeling was coming over Annabelle. She turned to Tiffany. "Do you know what?" With no humans in the house,

she didn't need to whisper, but she whispered anyway, because she was incredulous.

"No. What?" said Tiffany.

"I think this doll is the one who was supposed to come with our family instead of Baby Betsy," replied Annabelle. "I think she's my lost little sister."

CHAPTER TWO

Tilly May

"OH, NO," SAID TIFFANY. "She couldn't be your sister."

"Why not?" replied Annabelle. "I bet you anything that inside that box is a china baby doll with old-fashioned clothes like mine. The doll maker must have found her after he sent our family off to the United States, and realized he had included Baby Betsy instead of this doll. So he put Tilly in a box and he meant to mail her to William Cox, only that never happened. It sounds like the box fell somewhere and no one found it for a long time."

"Wellll," said Tiffany slowly, "I guess you could be right."

"I know I'm right. The doll in there is my sister. I can feel it."

Tiffany looked at the package. "Your parents are going to be awfully surprised."

"Mama and Papa!" exclaimed Annabelle. "I have to tell them right away! Just think how happy they'll be!"

"Shouldn't we let Tilly out?"

Annabelle hesitated. "Not without talking to the grown-ups first. Come on, Tiffany!" Annabelle ran partway along the couch, then turned and ran back to the package. "Tilly!" she called. "We're going to leave you for a while, but we'll be back as soon as we can, all right?"

"All right."

"I feel bad leaving her here," Annabelle said to Tiffany as they slid off the couch.

"Annabelle, if Tilly is who you think she is, she's been in that box for over a hundred years. A few more hours won't matter."

Nevertheless, Annabelle and Tiffany climbed the stairs to the second floor in record time and ran down the hall to Kate's room.

"Mama! Papa!" called Annabelle. She started up the step stool. *"Mama! Papa! Auntie Sarah! Uncle Doll! Everyone!"* she cried as loudly as she was able.

Uncle Doll appeared at the front of the house. He looked over the edge, wringing his hands. "Girls, are you all right?"

"Can you ask everyone to go to the parlor?" said Annabelle. "The most amazing thing has happened, and I want to tell all of you about it at once."

By the time Annabelle and Tiffany had flung themselves up over the top step and into the Dolls' parlor, Annabelle's entire family had gathered, as well as Tiffany's brother, Bailey.

"What happened? What happened?" said Bobby.

"Did you find something?" asked Bailey.

Annabelle made an effort to calm down. She wanted to tell her story in as organized a fashion as possible. "All right," she said. "Yes, something happened, and yes, we found something."

Tiffany, bouncing up and down on her toes, suddenly cried, "We found your long-lost baby!"

"What?" exclaimed Mama and Papa and Auntie Sarah and Nanny and Uncle Doll.

Bobby and Bailey looked at each other in disgust and said simultaneously, "You found a *baby*?"

Annabelle glared fiercely at Tiffany, then started at the beginning and told the others about the package and the address and Tilly May.

"Oh, but Annabelle, for pity's sake," said Mama. "Just because the doll is young and she comes from London doesn't mean she's the baby who was supposed to be part of our family." Mama looked protectively at Baby Betsy, who was propped up against the piano, her giant head lolling on the keys, occasionally causing one or another of them to plink.

"But she is, she must be," said Annabelle, and she explained again about the package that was meant to have been mailed to William Seaborn Cox, Esquire, so long ago.

"Nonsense," said Papa. "We have our very own baby right here."

"But there was a mix-up," said Tiffany.

"Betsy is from another doll set."

"No matter," said Mama firmly. "She's
our baby now."

"Well, even if you don't believe me,
there's still a live baby doll in that package, and
I think we should let her out. She's been—"
Annabelle started to say.

But Papa cut her off. "You will do no
such thing, either of you."

"I should say not," said Nanny.

"We can't even let her out?" exclaimed Annabelle.

"Absolutely not. That's just the kind of act that could put dollkind in jeopardy," said Papa. "What would the Palmers think when they came home and saw the box ripped open?"

"Well, they wouldn't know exactly what had happened," said Tiffany. "And they'd never think *we* did anything. They wouldn't know a doll had been in the package. I'm not even sure anyone except Mr. Palmer saw it."

"Grandma Katherine might figure it out," said Mama. "She might recognize the address of the shop."

Annabelle thought for a moment. "Then couldn't we just let Tilly out while the Palmers are away? There's a little rip in the paper. If we tore it—"

"If you *tore* it?!" repeated Uncle Doll, horrified. "If you tore it, you would do something you couldn't undo. You can't unrip a rip. That would be a serious offense, Annabelle. Especially if you did it on purpose." He paused, shaking his head. "You are dolls with *owners*," he went on. "That gives you extra responsibility. Dolls with owners have to be especially careful. Owners notice things other people might not."

"All right. What if we peeled back just enough tape to let Tilly out? That way, before the Palmers come back, we could return Tilly to the package and tape it up exactly the way it is now. It seems cruel to leave her sealed up when she knows we're here."

"Annabelle," said Mama. "No. I don't want you fiddling with that box. It's too dangerous, plain and simple. End of discussion."

"Mama, that's my sister in there. I know it," said Annabelle, and she felt very much as if she might begin to cry. But then, because she was also mad, she added, "And your daughter."

"Annabelle," said Mama.

"And yours, Papa." Annabelle turned to her aunt and uncle. "And your niece. And your sister," she said to Bobby. Annabelle let a small sob escape.

"Oh, dear," said Mama Doll, and she reached for Annabelle to give her a hug.

But Annabelle pulled away. "Come on," she said to Tiffany. And then, remembering something she had heard on the Palmers' television set once, she added, "We're not welcome here."

Tiffany, bewildered, turned and followed Annabelle down the stool. From behind her, she could hear Auntie Sarah say, "Let them go. Annabelle needs a chance to cool off."

Annabelle half ran and half stomped all the way back downstairs. "This is an outrage," she said (something else she had overheard) as she climbed onto the couch again. "It's incredible. Why won't Mama believe me?"

Tiffany paused before answering her friend. "Well, you have to admit," she said finally, "that it *is* hard to believe. I didn't believe you at first."

"I know." Annabelle sat down. She looked at the package, then leaned into the little rip and called, "Tilly May?"

"Yes?"

"It's me, Annabelle. I'm back."

"Hello."

"Hello." Annabelle sighed. Then she pulled Tiffany away from the package. "What do you suppose will happen when the Palmers come home?" she whispered.

"What do you mean?" Tiffany whispered back.

"I mean, if we leave Tilly here and they look at the package and decide it was sent to them by mistake, what will they do?"

"Oh," said Tiffany. And then, "Uh-oh. They might send it back without opening it. But," she continued slowly, "Grandma Katherine will probably know where the box is from. So will Mrs. Palmer."

"But they might *not* know," said Annabelle. "And if my little sister is in there, I can't let the Palmers send her back to London."

"No," said Tiffany slowly.

"I know what Mama and Papa said, but I

think we have to see if Tilly May truly is my sister."

"How will you be able to tell?"

"Partly by her face and by the clothes she's wearing. And partly . . . I'll just know."

Tiffany nodded.

"The Doll Code of Honor forbids us to

put dollkind in jeopardy," said Annabelle, "but there should be something in the code about protecting your family and your friends, shouldn't there? Like when we had to rescue Papa from The Captain."

"Yes. But there isn't anything like that."

Annabelle sighed again. Then she said, "Uncle Doll is right: you can't unrip a rip. But if we open the package so that we can seal it back up just as it was before, then we won't have broken the code."

Tiffany looked thoughtful.

"So I think we should at least peek inside. If we peel the tape carefully, the end of the package will open and we can let Tilly out. I hope."

"All right," said Tiffany.

Annabelle bounced back to the box and said to her friend, "If you take one end of the tape— here on this side—I'll take the other. Peel slowly, VERY slowly. Don't tear anything."

The girls worked hard.

Wilson and Sons
1 Scala Street
London, England

William
26 We
Reade, C

BY AIR MAIL
PRI avion
Royal Mail

It was a painstaking job. Annabelle and Tiffany peeled away for five long minutes before they had pulled off the entire strip. But when the last bit of tape came away from the paper, the end of the package opened up and Annabelle found herself looking in at the side of the box. Perfect.

"Tilly May!" called Annabelle, and she knocked on the box. "If you push right here from the inside and we pull from the outside, the end of the box will open."

And that is exactly what happened. Tilly May pushed, and Annabelle and Tiffany pulled, and the box opened so easily that

Annabelle and Tiffany fell backward onto the couch cushion. As they struggled to their feet they saw a small doll crawl out of the box, like a chick hatching from an egg. She stood unsteadily, peered up at Annabelle, and said, "Mama?"

"No, I'm Annabelle. Annabelle Doll. I think I'm your big sister."

Tilly turned to Tiffany. "Mama?"

Tiffany shook her head. "Sorry. I'm Tiffany Funcraft, Annabelle's friend."

"Is my mama here?" asked Tilly.

Annabelle winced. "Um, no."

"Okay," said Tilly, and she sat down on the couch with a little plop.

Tiffany grabbed Annabelle's hand. "I can't believe it!" she exclaimed softly. "She does look like you!"

Annabelle studied Tilly May. Tilly's long white dress was trimmed with pink, and on her head was a white lace-edged bonnet that tied under her chin with a pink bow. Her face was Annabelle's face, her hands were Annabelle's hands, her feet were Annabelle's feet. If she had been taller, she might have been mistaken for Annabelle herself. Except for her hair. Tilly's hair was a nice shade of yellow. Annabelle's was green, and had been since Grandma Katherine was six years old and had decided to give Annabelle a new hair color. Grandma Katherine's mother, Gertrude, had tried to remove the green, but had been only partially successful.

"Well," whispered Annabelle, "what are we going to do now?"

"With Tilly May?" Tiffany whispered back, and Annabelle nodded. "Hmm. We have two more weeks until the Palmers come home. At least she's out of the box. We can hide her downstairs if we have to. But I don't think your parents are going to come down here, so—"

"That's not what I mean," said Annabelle. "I mean, now that we know she's my little sister, I can't just put her back in the package when the Palmers come home. What if they decide the box wasn't meant for them, and they send it back without opening it? That can't happen, Tiffany. I can't let it. Imagine how horrible it would be for Tilly May. Imagine how scared she'd be!"

"Okay. Calm down. We'll think of something."

"Like what?"

"I don't know. Give me a minute. You have to think too, Annabelle."

"I can't concentrate." Annabelle looked at Tilly, who was sitting on the couch, gazing around the Palmers' living room.

"This is a big box," said Tilly.

"What?" said Annabelle.

"This is a very big box we're in."

"This isn't a box," Annabelle told her sister. "This is a room."

"What's a room?"

Annabelle gulped. Her sister didn't even know what a room was. She'd been trapped in a box for a hundred years and knew only darkness, tissue paper, and six cardboard walls.

"Tiffany, this is terrible," said Annabelle. "Tilly thinks this room is just another box. That's been her whole world. A box. And Mama and Papa want to *leave* her in the box. And then maybe lose her forever."

"All right, all right. Let's think this through. Say that when the Palmers come home they decide to send the package back."

"Okay."

"So they take it to the post office and mail it to London."

"Okay."

"And it's returned to the person who mailed it in the first place."

"Okay."

"What do you think that person would do with the package?"

"I don't know! He could do anything! But whatever he did, Tilly May would be there, not here, and I want my little sister!" Annabelle's voice rose to a wail.

"The thing is," said Tiffany, "I'm not sure we have a lot of choices. We can either put Tilly back in the box before the Palmers come home, or we can leave her out and try to hide her—forever—which I think is really dangerous."

Annabelle was silent. Tiffany was one of the bravest doll people she knew. Annabelle pictured her friend floating in the bathtub with Nora, being tossed through the air, being shoved across the floor in a rackety metal truck, and made to ride plastic cows and horses. If Tiffany thought tampering with the box and hiding Tilly was dangerous, well then . . .

"All right," said Annabelle finally. "There's only one thing to do."

"What?" said Tiffany.

"I'll have to take Tilly and run away."

Tiffany sat down with a thump. "Annabelle, you can't!"

Annabelle saw the shock on her friend's

face and was stricken. But she couldn't take her words back. "I have to," she said again.

"But what will happen after the Palmers' vacation when Kate looks and looks for you and can't find you?"

"I don't know," said Annabelle.

"And then the Palmers discover that the package is empty," Tiffany went on, "and they know The Captain can't be responsible this time. Annabelle, you'll put your whole family in danger. You'll put all of us in danger."

"But you can look out for yourselves," Annabelle replied. "And Tilly can't. She's little." Annabelle's eyes wandered to the window. "Wow, it's already morning. I'd better get going. Mama and Papa won't be expecting me for a while, since they know I'm so mad; but sooner or later they'll get worried and come looking for me, and I want to get a head start." She held out her hand. "Come on, Tilly."

Tilly struggled to her feet and took her sister's hand. "Where are we going?" she asked.

"On a big adventure." Annabelle led her sister to the edge of the couch.

Tiffany, balancing on a couch cushion, looked at her best friend, poised to disappear over the edge of the sofa. "Wait!" called Tiffany. "Wait! Annabelle, if you're going to run away, I'm coming with you."

CHAPTER THREE

The Runaways

"**B**UT BEFORE WE GO," said Tiffany, "we ought to seal the package up so that it looks the same as it did when the Palmers last saw it. Tilly's so light, they'll never know the package is empty."

"Unless they open it," replied Annabelle grimly. "That's good thinking, though," she added, and she and Tiffany closed the end of the box, patted the paper back in place, and sealed it with the tape.

"How does that look?" asked Annabelle.

Tiffany surveyed their work. "Great," she

said. "We could become thieves. All right. Let's get going."

"Uh-oh," cried Annabelle. "How are we going to get out of the house? We can't open any of the doors. How would we turn the knobs?"

"We'll find a door we can pull open from the bottom," said Tiffany. "Like the attic door."

Annabelle and Tiffany had spent a good deal of time in the attic of the Palmers' house. They had had many adventures up there, including finding Auntie Sarah after she had been lost for forty-five years. And their journeys always began by wriggling their hands under the crack beneath the door to the attic stairs (which didn't latch properly) and swinging it open.

"All right," said Annabelle, and the dolls set off.

Traveling with Tilly May turned out to

be rather difficult. For one thing, she was smaller than Annabelle and Tiffany, so her legs were shorter, which meant that she couldn't move as fast as they could. For another, she stopped every few inches to ask a question.

"What's that?" she said as they passed a chair leg.

"What's that?" she said as they passed a boot.

"What's that?" she said as they passed a cat toy, an umbrella, a sneaker, a backpack, a baseball bat, a dish, a doormat.

Annabelle tried to answer each question patiently, but some things were hard to explain. For instance, "That's a cat toy," she said.

"What's a cat toy?" Tilly wanted to know.

"Well, a toy is something you play with," said Annabelle.

"Oh. What's a cat?"

"Should we show her The Captain?" asked Tiffany.

"No!" shrieked Annabelle. "Anyway, here's the front door. But there's no crack under it, and it's closed tight."

"Back door, then," said Tiffany.

"What's that?" asked Tilly May, pointing into a corner.

"It's a dust bunny," replied Annabelle.

"What's a dust bunny?"

"A bunny is a kind of animal," said Annabelle, "but a *dust* bunny is . . . well, it's a collection of hair and dust."

"What's an animal?" asked Tilly. "What's a collection?"

Annabelle was exhausted.

"Okay, here's the back door," said Tiffany. "No crack under it either."

So far, running away was not going well.

"I know!" said Annabelle suddenly. "The Captain's door! We can go out the cat door. It's close to the ground and you can push through it. I've seen The Captain do that lots of times. And we won't have to worry about The Captain, since he's closed in the kitchen."

"Oh, brilliant!" cried Tiffany. "Annabelle, you're a genius."

Annabelle was pleased with herself, although she didn't particularly feel like a genius.

"How many more minutes?" asked Tilly suddenly.

"How many more minutes until what?" replied Tiffany.

And Annabelle said, "How do you know what minutes are, Tilly? In fact, how do you know anything?"

"From listening," said Tilly.

"Listening to what?" asked Annabelle.

"The fing called the radio."

"The radio? Was there a radio in the doll maker's shop?"

"Somewhere it was," said Tilly. "I could hear it all the times. Well, not *all* the times. But lots and lots and lots of times."

"She's been listening to the radio. For years and years," Annabelle exclaimed softly to Tiffany.

"That explains a few things."

The dolls were running through the Palmers' hallway toward the back of the house. Tilly asked again, "How many more minutes?"

"Until *what*?" asked Tiffany, sounding exasperated.

"Until we get to the cat door fing."

"I don't know. Why?"

Tilly stopped and looked down at her legs, then asked, "Are we running?"

Annabelle stopped too. "Tiffany," she said, "Tilly's been cooped up in that box since the end of the nineteenth century. She's probably never had so much exercise."

"You'd think she be glad to be running around."

"Yes, but her legs aren't used to it. She's actually kind of like a newborn baby. Except that she can talk." Annabelle turned to her sister. "Tilly, do you need to rest?"

"My legs want to hold still."

Tiffany and Annabelle sat on the hallway rug with Tilly May, who kept losing her balance and toppling over. At last Tiffany said, "Listen, I hear the clock. Let's count the chimes and see what time it is. I really think we should get going, Annabelle."

"I can count," announced Tilly May, sitting up again. "Ten," she said, "nine, eight, seven, six, five—"

"You're counting backward," said Tiffany.

"—four, free, two, one, happy new year!"

"That's great, Tilly," said Annabelle, and she put her arm around her sister.

Tiffany cocked her head, listening. "It's nine o'clock already."

"Tilly, do you think you can walk some more?" asked Annabelle. "It's only a little farther to the cat door."

Tilly fell over again, then stood up. "All right. Let's go."

The Captain's door was at the side of the house, and consisted of a hinged flap that swung back and forth from the top of a small rectangular opening. The opening, which Mrs. Palmer worried about ("What if a raccoon gets into the house? Or a squirrel or a possum?") was just big enough for The Captain, and plenty big enough for the dolls. When they reached it, Annabelle gave a tentative push and saw a flash of sunlight on the other side of the door.

"It works," she said to Tiffany. And suddenly she felt very nervous. She had never voluntarily left the safety of the humans' house. She and Tiffany had been out of doors—they had had one memorable adventure in which they had accidentally gone to school in Kate's backpack, and then to a boy's house, where they had met Mean Mimi—but they hadn't left on purpose. And now that's exactly what they were about to do.

Annabelle pushed the door open and looked out into the sunlight again. Then she drew her head back inside and said to Tiffany, "I know running away was my idea, but do you think we should really do it?"

"Oh, Annabelle."

"I have a good idea what's going to happen when everyone figures out that we've run away."

"How will they figure out that we've run away?"

"Like this," said Annabelle. "You see, Auntie Sarah understands me better than anyone does. Except you," she added loyally. "She knows I was mad. And I think she believes that Tilly May really is the missing baby. At least she understands that *I* believe she's the missing baby. So when we don't come back, I'm pretty sure she'll decide we ran away with Tilly. And then Mama and Papa will get upset, and Auntie Sarah will defend me, and Mama and Papa will say that Auntie Sarah *always* defends me, and then eventually all the grown-ups will be mad at Auntie Sarah.

Except for Uncle Doll. He'll just sulk, and soon their whole vacation will be ruined.

"I wish my parents could be a little more relaxed," Annabelle continued. "Like your parents. When your parents realize you're gone, they'll miss you and everything, but they won't get upset. They'll just hope you have a good adventure. Won't they?"

"At first," said Tiffany. "But if we're gone for a *really* long time, they'll get worried too."

Annabelle sighed. Then she poked her head through the cat door a third time. When she did, she found herself face-to-face with a grasshopper.

"Aughhh!" shrieked Annabelle, and ducked back inside.

"What? What?" asked Tiffany.

"A giant green . . . grasshopper, I think. This might be a bad—" Annabelle suddenly stopped speaking. "Tiffany, where's Tilly May?"

Annabelle and Tiffany looked around the hallway. No Tilly.

Then Tiffany cocked her head. "Listen," she said.

Annabelle listened intently. From beyond

the cat door came the sound of laughter. Annabelle poked her head outside. Tilly was sitting in the sunshine, a tiny, tiny doll among tall blades of grass, like a rabbit in a forest. Behind her was the Palmers' driveway, which until this moment Annabelle had glimpsed only from Kate's window. To her left were trees reaching so high into the sky that Annabelle had to lean over backward to see the tops of them. The grasshopper had disappeared, but perched on the toe of one of Tilly's shoes was a shiny red-and-black ladybug, and it was the ladybug that was making Tilly laugh.

"Annabelle!" said Tilly. "This is the best box I have ever been in!" She pointed to the ladybug. "What's that?" she asked.

"It's a ladybug," said Annabelle.

"And what's that?"

"A tree."

"What's that?"

"A pebble."

Annabelle regarded Tiffany, who had followed her through the cat door. "All right. We have to leave," she said. "Look how happy Tilly is. She deserves to see what's outside the box."

Annabelle turned her face to the sun. She didn't know what was going to happen next. She didn't know where she and Tiffany and Tilly May were headed, or even in which direction they should set off.

But we're going to leave, and leave right now, thought Annabelle resolutely. "Come on," she said. She took her sister by one hand, and Tiffany took Tilly by the other, and they led her toward the driveway, where most of the Palmers' adventures began.

CHAPTER FOUR

A Daring Rescue

"Now what?" said Tiffany when the dolls were standing at the edge of the Palmers' driveway.

Annabelle looked down the drive to the street. A car flew by. She looked behind the Palmers' house at the woods. She looked across the yard to the yellow house next door. The house belonged to Mrs. Kay Robinson and her husband. (Mrs. Robinson was responsible for feeding The Captain while

the Palmers were away. Earlier, she had let herself in the back door to give The Captain his breakfast.) Annabelle considered the bleeding hearts by the front door, and the brick path leading to the stoop, but they didn't give her any ideas about running away. She looked across the driveway at the house belonging to the Myerses, the Palmers' next-door neighbors on the other side. There were the Myers boys, Jonah and William, whom Kate and Nora claimed to hate. They didn't give Annabelle any ideas either.

At last she turned to Tiffany. "I guess," she said slowly, "that we should start by running down the driveway to the sidewalk."

"In the daylight?" said Tiffany. "Don't you think we should stay out of sight?"

"But we're so small, and everything is so big. No one will notice us. Anyway, we'll be careful."

Tiffany looked doubtful. "Okay," she said finally. "Stick to the edge, though, so we can duck into that garden if we have to."

A row of peony bushes lined one side of the driveway. Annabelle and Tiffany, with Tilly May between them, hurried along under the canopy of leaves until they reached the sidewalk.

"Now what?" said Tiffany again. "Where are we going?"

"Um," said Annabelle, "back to school?"

"To Kate and Nora's school?" said Tiffany.

"What's a school?" asked Tilly May, who had taken advantage of the pause to sit down on a peony petal.

Annabelle thought for a moment. "It's a big building where—"

"What's a building?" interrupted Tilly May.

Annabelle drew in a breath and let it out very slowly. Silently she counted to ten. "Tilly," she said, "I know everything is new to you, and I know you're happy to be out of the box."

"Yes," agreed Tilly.

"But I can't answer all your questions. Not right now. Tiffany and I need to think. Could you store up your questions and ask them later?"

"What does 'store up' mean?"

Annabelle pursed her lips, then said

patiently, "It means 'save.' Please save your questions for a while."

"All right," said Tilly, and she busied herself making a peony petal hat.

"Why do you want to go to the school?" Tiffany asked Annabelle.

"I don't know. I guess because we've been there before."

"Do you think the school is open? After all, it's summer vacation."

Annabelle, voice trembling, said, "Oh, never mind. It was a silly idea. We don't even know how to get to the school. The last time we went, we traveled in Kate's backpack. We couldn't see where we were going."

"Now wait. Don't get upset," said Tiffany. "We'll think of something."

"Where do people go when they run away?"

Tiffany looked thoughtful. "Well, Dorothy Gale wound up in Oz. And the Darlings wound up in Never Land."

"The Darlings didn't actually run away, though," Annabelle pointed out.

"And anyway, those are all book characters, not real people. Or real doll people. I wonder where *people* go when they run away."

Annabelle shook her head. "I don't know. Maybe they don't know either. I mean, maybe they don't know when they start out. Maybe they just . . . go."

"Then I think," said Tiffany, "that we should go wherever our feet carry us."

Annabelle stood up and turned in a circle, looking all around her. That was when she heard voices.

"Come on!" called Jonah Myers. "Hurry up! I want to have time to go swimming later."

"I *am* hurrying," replied his brother. "But we have a ton of stuff to deliver today."

Annabelle now saw that Jonah and William were dropping armloads of bundles into two red wagons parked outside their front door. She looked at Tiffany and put her finger to her lips, and then she and Tiffany each grabbed Tilly by an arm. They dove into the peony bushes.

"Did they see us?" whispered Annabelle.

Tiffany shook her head. "No."

"I wonder what they're doing."

"I know what they're doing. I heard Kate and Nora talking about it. Jonah and William started their own business this summer. Myers Flyers. Someone will call them and say, 'We need a hundred flyers to advertise our patio furniture sale.' Jonah and William ask what the flyers should look like and what information to include, and then they create them on their computer and print them out. I guess today they're delivering the flyers they've made."

Annabelle peered through the screen of peony leaves. "Tiffany," she said softly, "I have an idea. If we could get in one of the wagons, we could hitch a ride. Who knows where we might end up. Anywhere! It would be a real adventure."

"Gosh," said Tiffany, "I don't know."

"We'll go a lot faster in the wagon than if we try to walk with Tilly."

The boys disappeared inside their house, and Annabelle suddenly burst out of the garden, pulling Tilly behind her. "Hurry!" she called to Tiffany.

The dolls ran as fast as their tiny legs would move, Annabelle half dragging Tilly. They were standing just three feet from the wagons when the door opened again and out came Jonah and William.

"Garden!" said Tiffany in a frantic whisper, and she launched herself behind a birdbath in the Myerses' flower bed.

Annabelle scurried next to her, one hand clapped over Tilly's mouth, silently urging the boys to make another trip inside.

"One last load," said William then, and Annabelle breathed a sigh of relief. When the door closed behind the boys, she ran for the nearer of the wagons, scrambled up one wheel, and fell over the edge onto the packages.

"Grab Tilly!" said Tiffany, holding her aloft, and Annabelle took her sister's hands and hauled her into the wagon. Tiffany tumbled in after them, and the dolls crawled between two teetering stacks of papers. Moments later they felt the wagon start to move, jouncing across the lawn to the sidewalk.

"Oh," said Tilly May, "I don't like this box."

"I hope she doesn't get carsick," said Tiffany. "I mean, wagonsick."

"Shh," said Annabelle, although she didn't really think the boys could hear them over the rattling and banging of the wagon wheels.

They rumbled along for what seemed a very long time. Annabelle was tempted to stand up and peer over the edge, but she knew better than to risk being seen. At last the wagon jerked to a halt, and Annabelle heard one of the boys say, "First stop, Sweet Lisa's." Then a hand reached into the wagon and removed one of the bundles.

"I *have* to find out where we are," said Tiffany when the boys had left. She stood on her tiptoes. "I see lots of buildings close together," she reported to Annabelle and Tilly. "And lots of people, all in a hurry. And cars and trucks. You know where I think we are, Annabelle?"

Annabelle nodded. "Downtown." It was a place she had only heard about.

Jonah and William returned then and continued making their deliveries. Annabelle winced each time they removed a bundle from the wagon. Their hiding places were disappearing.

The dolls were huddled in a back corner when a splash of water landed on Annabelle's head, then on her hand, and then on her shoe. "Oh, no!" she whispered. "It's raining!"

"I hope it doesn't thunder," replied Tiffany.

"What's funder?" asked Tilly.

"Shh. Never mind."

"William, we'd better go home for a while," Jonah said to his brother. "We didn't bring an umbrella. And we don't want any of the flyers to get wet."

"We don't have time!" cried William. "Now it's really raining. Quick! Into the woods. It'll be dryer under the trees."

The wagon jerked forward, then flew along so fast that Annabelle and Tiffany and Tilly were flung about as if they had accidentally been tossed in a washing machine, which Tiffany confessed later had actually happened to her once. When the wagon came to a sudden stop, the dolls were thrown forward into the bundles of paper.

Tilly began to wail.

"Hush!" said Annabelle. "Tilly, you can't make any noise." She turned to Tiffany and whispered, "She has so much to learn."

"At least it isn't a thunderstorm," said Tiffany.

"Jonah!" William called, and the other wagon stopped rattling along. "Let's stay under this tree for a while. It's totally dry here."

Annabelle dared to peep over the edge of the wagon. She stared about, then dropped back down to Tilly and Tiffany. "You won't believe it!" she whispered. "You should see where we are. It's—it's a magic forest. Nothing but trees and flowers."

"I think it's just a regular forest," said Tiffany. "We're in the town park."

"Well, it looks magic. It's all peaceful, with the rain dripping down here and there. And the trees—they're even bigger when you see them up close. They're forest giants. And listen. Listen to the sounds."

The dolls sat still and listened. They could hear the pattering of rain on leaves, and the chirping of crickets (a sound with which Annabelle and Tiffany had become familiar during their terrifying adventure at the boy's house), and lots and lots of birds calling to one another.

"Chickadee!" said Tilly May. "Chickadee-dee-dee." She paused, then said,

"Oh, a robin. And a catbird! That's a catbird!"

"Tilly, shh," said Annabelle. But then she whispered, "How do you know birdcalls?"

"From a tape fing."

"Someone played a tape of birdcalls?" said Tiffany.

"I fink so. Birds Around the World."

"Hey, William!" shouted Jonah. "Look what I found!"

Annabelle stiffened. For one horrifying moment she expected a human hand to reach in and pluck her out of the wagon. But then Jonah said, "It's a snake skin. A whole snake skin. Let's go see if we can find the snake it came off of."

When the crashing footsteps had faded away, and the dolls had heard nothing but cricket chirps and birdcalls for several minutes, Tiffany said, "Let's have a better look around. Climb up on the papers. You can use them like steps."

Annabelle and Tilly followed Tiffany, and they rested their arms on the edge of the wagon and gazed at the woods.

"Uh-oh," said Tilly May.

"What's wrong?" asked Annabelle.

"My bonnet. It fell off."

Annabelle looked at the ground below and saw the tiny white bonnet lying by the wagon wheel.

"Let it go," said Tiffany.

"No!" Tilly glared at Tiffany. "I *like* my bonnet," she said fiercely.

"Okay, okay, we'll get it for you. Come help me, Annabelle. It will be quicker that way. You stay here, Tilly."

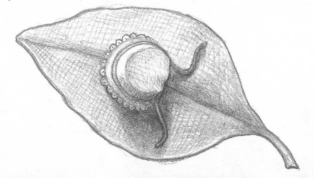

Annabelle and Tiffany scrambled out of the wagon, and Annabelle reached for the bonnet.

"I told you we wouldn't find the snake."

Tiffany jumped. Annabelle let out a tiny shriek.

"The boys are back!" squeaked Tiffany. "Quick. Hide!"

But before the dolls could find a hiding spot, the wagons started to roll away through the woods.

Annabelle stared at them in horror, searching desperately for a glimpse of her sister. "It already stopped raining," she heard William say, his voice trailing off among the trees. "We can go back to town now."

"After them!" shouted Tiffany.

Annabelle ran and ran, pounding along behind Tiffany, who was both faster and sturdier than she was. But after only a minute, Tiffany slowed down and then stopped. She turned to Annabelle. "We can't catch them," she said.

"You've never given up before," replied Annabelle in surprise. "Never."

"I'm not giving up," said Tiffany. "But look." She indicated the wagons, which were now so far away, the dolls could barely hear them.

Annabelle slumped to the ground, not caring that she'd landed in a patch of very damp grass. "This is my fault," she whispered. "All my fault."

"Well . . ." said Tiffany.

"No. Don't try to make me feel better. There's nothing you can say. I was the one who wanted to run away. I was the one who disobeyed my parents. I was the one who thought we could take care of Tilly. And now everything is ruined."

Annabelle put her

head in
her hands.

"So you're
just going to sit there and
feel sorry for yourself?"
asked Tiffany.

Annabelle glanced up at
her friend. "No . . . I guess
not."

"Because I really don't
see what good that's going
to do."

Annabelle squared
her shoulders.
"You're right,"
she said. "We

have to do something. It's just that . . ."

"What?" asked Tiffany.

"I don't know what it is we should do."

"For one thing," said Tiffany, "we need to think clearly. Remember SELMP?"

"SELMP!" exclaimed Annabelle. "Of course."

When Auntie Sarah had been missing, which now seemed like ages and ages ago, Annabelle and Tiffany had formed SELMP, the Society for Exploration and the Location of Missing Persons. If they were going to be good explorers, Tiffany had reasoned, then they needed to form an official organization dedicated to exploring in general, and to finding missing doll people in particular. They hadn't had much use for SELMP after they had located Auntie Sarah, but now Annabelle saw that it was exactly what they needed.

"Okay," said Annabelle. "We will think clearly and make a plan. There are lots of things we need to do, but the most important one is to find Tilly. After that we need to get home again, and then we'll need to figure out what to do with Tilly."

"But first things first," said Tiffany, quoting Auntie Sarah.

"Right. First things first." Annabelle pointed to the ground. "We can follow the tracks."

And so Annabelle Doll and Tiffany Funcraft set out after the wagons, trotting beside the ruts the wheels had made in the damp earth. It was really rather exciting, Annabelle realized. Here she was, outdoors among actual living trees and flowers and insects, things that so far she knew only from books or from seeing them on the Palmers' television. Grass was *soft*, Annabelle discovered. So were flower petals. Tree bark was rough. And sunshine was very bright when you were actually standing in it.

Annabelle became so engrossed in these thoughts that at first she didn't notice the three small figures that appeared in the distance.

"Annabelle?" said Tiffany. And then, "Annabelle! Look!"

Annabelle pulled her thoughts away from flower petals and sunshine. "What? Where?"

"*There!*" Tiffany pointed ahead to a spot

where the wagon tracks were lost from sight behind a jagged rock.

Annabelle squinted her eyes. Hurrying toward her down the tracks was Tilly May. And she was hand in hand with Bobby and Bailey.

CHAPTER FIVE

Bobby and Bailey

ANNABELLE HIKED UP the hem of her dress and, holding it off the ground, ran through the woods, her feet slurping in the mud. "Bobby!" she cried. "Bailey! What are you *doing* here? And how did you find Tilly?" Annabelle scooped her sister into her arms and hugged her tightly.

Tiffany slowed to a stop and stared at the boys. For once she was speechless.

"Surprised?" said Bailey.

"I—" Tiffany paused. "Where are the Myers boys? Where are the wagons? How did you get Tilly *out* of the wagon?"

"And how did you get *here*?" asked Annabelle. But before the boys could answer, she set Tilly down, tied the bonnet on her head, and hugged first Bobby (who squirmed from her grasp), and then Bailey (who muttered "yuck").

Bobby turned to Tiffany. "Aren't you glad to see us?" he asked.

"Of course she is," Annabelle answered. "We just weren't expecting you."

"You got yourselves into a little bit of trouble, didn't you?" said Bailey.

"Well, yes," Annabelle said sheepishly.

"I have a feeling we're *all* in trouble now," added Tiffany. "Even . . . T.M." She nodded in the direction of Tilly May.

Annabelle, suddenly conscious of her muddy clothing, sat down on a flat rock and spread her skirts around her so they could dry in the sun. "You'd better tell us everything," she said to the boys. "From the very beginning."

"All right," Bobby replied, and he and Bailey and Tiffany and Tilly joined Annabelle on the rock, Tilly climbing into her sister's lap.

"The thing is," Bailey began, "Bobby and I have been spying on you girls."

"For days," added Bobby.

"So *that's* what you've been up to!" exclaimed Tiffany. "We knew you were doing something. How come you were spying on us?"

"Just for fun," said Bailey. "Except it didn't really get interesting until after you found Tilly May. You girls sure can be boring."

Tiffany waved at her brother as if he were an annoying mosquito. "Okay, okay. So you were spying on us, and . . . ?"

"We followed you out the cat door this morning," said Bobby.

"You have to admit that going out the cat door was hardly boring," said Tiffany.

"Then we hid in the bushes while you figured out what to do."

"We couldn't believe it when you climbed into the wagon," added Bailey. "We thought we'd better come with you in case you needed us—which you did."

"But where were you?" asked Annabelle.

"In the other wagon. We spied on you all morning."

"How did you get Tilly?"

"Easy," said Bobby, with a toss of his head. "Jonah and William stopped to explore a creek. So we jumped out of our wagon and got Tilly out of the other one, and then we just followed the tracks back to you." He paused. "Um, Annabelle? Now that I've seen her up close, I know you're right. I know Tilly is our sister."

Bobby looked as though he was going to say something else, but Bailey was muttering something about girls and mush, so Bobby clamped his mouth shut.

Annabelle smiled at her brother. "Thank heavens you were spying on us," she said. "But now what are we going to do?"

"What do you *want* to do?" asked Bobby. "I mean, where do you want to go?"

"Do you still want to run away?" asked Bailey, looking hopeful.

"No!" cried Annabelle. "We have to get home. Running away was a terrible idea. Too dangerous. I don't know what I was thinking."

"But we're going to be in so much trouble," said Bailey.

"Not if we find our way back today," said Annabelle. "If we get home before dark, how much trouble could we be in? The grown-ups will barely have missed us."

"I hate to say this, but there's no way we're going to get home today." Bobby was studying the sun in the sky. "It's after lunch now, and we've probably traveled two miles. Unless those wagons come back this way, we won't be home for a long, long time. The wagons move fast, but we can't."

"Our legs are short," spoke up Tilly.

"I think," said Tiffany, "that we should walk as far as we can before it gets dark, and then if we're still in the woods, we'll stop somewhere for the night."

"What if"—Annabelle shivered—"what if we *never* get out of these woods?"

"Well, that's just ridiculous," said Tiffany. "It isn't as if we're in the wilderness. We're in a park."

"There might be wild animals here."

"Oh!" cried Tilly May. "Wild Animal Sound Track, Tape One! Tiger—*grrrrr*. Hyena—"

"What?" said Bailey, frowning.

"I'll explain later," Annabelle replied.

"Well, anyway," said Bobby, "the only wild animals we're going to find in the park are squirrels and chipmunks."

"That's not true," said Annabelle. "Jonah and William saw a snake skin. And there are birds here, and—"

"What about bats?" said Bailey. "I bet there'll be bats out tonight. I've always wanted to see a bat."

"Bats! Oh, no, no," said Annabelle with a small moan. "A bat is big enough to pick one of us up in its mouth—its furry little mouth with those horrid sharp fangs—and swoop away—"

"They're not going to see us. Bats are *blind*, silly," said Tiffany. "That's why people say 'blind as a bat.'"

"Actually," said Bobby. "That's just a saying. Big bats aren't blind—"

"Bats have radar," Annabelle interrupted him. "They use it to zero in on insects."

"I hardly think we're going to be mistaken for insects!" Tiffany exclaimed.

"Okay, okay," interrupted Bobby. "You're getting off the subject. The point is that we are not going to make it home today. Also, we'll probably have to spend the night in the woods."

"All right. Let's think," said Annabelle. She looked at her brother and sister and friends. They were still gathered on the flat rock. Around them were stiff blades of grass, dusty green leaves, and a carpet of something with a sharp but pleasant smell that Annabelle thought might be pine needles. Then Annabelle looked just beyond the rock to the trees, the trees that seemed impossibly large to a small doll sitting beneath them.

I don't care if we are in a town park, thought Annabelle. This feels like the wilderness. I could be Laura Ingalls in the big woods. Or I could be Gretel, lost in the forest.

Hansel and Gretel was one of the scariest stories Annabelle had ever heard, but it had once been Kate's favorite, so Annabelle, posed rigidly in her house, had been forced to listen to it over and over again while Grandma Katherine or Mr. or Mrs. Palmer had read it to Kate at bedtime.

Annabelle pulled her thoughts back. Concentrate, she told herself. What are we going to do? We can't leave a trail like Hansel and Gretel did. It's already too late for that.

Bobby cleared his throat. "I have some ideas," he said.

"You do?" replied Annabelle in surprise.

"Yes. Don't you?"

"No. Why should I?"

"Because of what Kate learned in school this spring. You know, her nature unit? On outdoor survival skills? All that stuff she was telling Nora about every afternoon?"

Annabelle wrinkled her nose. "I didn't pay attention to any of that. It didn't sound very interesting."

"Not very interesting! But she was learning about poisonous mushrooms and hypothermia."

"And snakebites!" added Bailey. "I got to hear some of it once."

"Tell us what you learned," said Tiffany to Bobby.

"Well, a lot of it doesn't matter to us," he admitted. "We don't need to eat or drink anything, so we don't have to forage for food or look for potable water. That means water that's safe to drink. And we can't get frostbite or hypothermia. Even a snakebite won't do anything to us."

"Except terrify us," muttered Annabelle. "Plus, a snake could swallow any one of us whole."

"Annabelle, I really don't think that's our biggest worry."

"Did you hear Kate say anything about finding your way home when you're lost?" asked Bailey.

"Yes," replied Bobby, sounding quite confident. "First of all, we should mark this place—the rock, I guess—somehow, so that if we see it again later on we'll know we've been traveling in a circle. Second, we should keep track of the sun so we can try to travel in one direction and *not* go in circles."

"Okay," said Annabelle, impressed.

"Now the first thing I think we need to decide is whether to follow Jonah and William, or to retrace our steps and go back the way we came."

"We'd better follow Jonah and William, don't you think?" spoke up Tiffany. "If we go back, we'll wind up downtown again, and we have no idea how we got there."

"And if we follow the boys," said

Annabelle, "we might even catch up with them. For all we know, they're still exploring the creek. We could sneak back into one of the wagons. Maybe we won't have to spend the night out here after all."

"That's true," replied Tiffany.

"Raise your hand if you want to follow the boys," said Bobby.

He and Bailey and Annabelle and Tiffany raised their hands. Tilly May had found an old acorn cap and was spinning around in it. "Fun!" she cried.

"Four in favor," said Bailey. "That's a majority."

Tiffany got to her feet. "Let's go, then."

The dolls slid off the rock, and Bobby suggested marking it by placing a ring of pebbles in the center. Then, single file, they followed the wagon tracks through the woods.

"What's that?" asked Tilly as they passed a dandelion.

"What's that?" she asked as they passed a blue jay feather.

"What's that?" she asked as they passed a tree stump, a spider, an earthworm.

Annabelle tried to answer her sister as they marched along among the trees.

CHAPTER SIX

Pioneers

THE FARTHER THE DOLLS walked, the darker the woods became.

"What time is it?" Annabelle asked her brother. "Is it evening already?"

Bobby looked at the sky. He shook his head. "Nope. But I think it's going to rain again."

"Oh, dear."

"What's that?" asked Tilly May as they passed a fern.

"Oh, please. Make her stop," Bailey whispered to Annabelle.

"Tilly, maybe you could play the quiet game," said Tiffany.

"What's the quiet game?" asked Tilly.

"It's when you see how long you can walk through the woods without talking. Only girl dolls who are three years old are allowed to play."

"Oh!" cried Tilly. "That's me! I'm free years—"

Tiffany put her finger to her lips. "Shh! You don't want to lose the game."

Tilly May closed her mouth and trotted along beside her sister.

Annabelle kept her eyes on the tracks. So far they were easy to follow. "What are some other things you learned from Kate?" she asked Bobby. "What was the most interesting thing?"

Bobby considered the question. "Well," he said finally, "Kate mentioned that Canadian Army Arctic parkas come with survival buttons you can eat."

"Why do you eat the button fings?" asked Tilly.

"Shh! Quiet game," said Tiffany.

"The buttons," said Bobby, "are made of a special protein that can be cooked in water to create a kind of emergency food."

"Cool!" said Bailey.

"Are the jackets still warm after the buttons are gone?" asked Tiffany.

Bobby ignored the question. "Of course, survival buttons wouldn't help *us*," he added. "But, well, one day we might need that information to rescue one of the Palmers."

"A doll rescuing a human!" exclaimed Annabelle. "I don't think so."

"You never know," said Bobby. "Anything is possible."

"Anyfing—" Tilly started to say.

"SHH!" said Tiffany.

"We never thought we'd be out here by ourselves in the woods," Bobby continued. "Or that we'd find our baby sister a hundred years later."

"That's true," Annabelle conceded, but privately she thought that a doll rescuing a human from any situation was highly unlikely. Still, she admired her brother's imagination and determination.

"Here's another interesting fact," said Bobby, turning his face to the sky. "An *ice blink* is a white glare on the underside of clouds that lets you know there's ice present on land when you can't even see it." He paused. "And *prevailing winds* have to do with global circulation patterns, things like the trade winds and jet streams. Then there's animal tracking."

Annabelle shuddered and had to stop listening to her brother. Animal tracking made her think of animals, which made her think of snakes and then bats, and bats made her think of the nighttime, which reminded her that she would probably be sleeping in these woods that night; sleeping out in the open with the bats and snakes and any number of creatures close at hand, hidden from her by the dark. She imagined sitting under a tree or a toadstool, hearing a small sound, and suddenly becoming aware of two glowing eyes. Annabelle almost screamed, but stopped herself and thought instead of her own bed in the nursery in the Dolls' house. If she ever got home, she would never leave again. Ever. (Probably.)

Bobby ran out of facts, and the dolls walked on silently.

"I have to lose the game," said Tilly suddenly.

Tiffany let out an enormous sigh. "Why?"

"I have to ask about the spots on my dress."

Annabelle looked at her sister's formerly white dress. "That's mud," she said. "Those spots are mud."

"Mud," repeated Tilly.

"And I hope it washes out. I'm muddy too. So is Bobby."

"Is that a bad fing?"

"Maybe."

Mud could put Annabelle and her brother and sister in Doll State. If the Palmers returned from their trips, and Kate found her dolls wearing clothing that was dirty and torn, she wouldn't be able to blame it on Nora and one of her games of Rancher Family or Miami Beach-a-go-go. She wouldn't be able to blame it on The Captain or on anything at all, and she would become suspicious, and . . . Oh, dear. This was assuming the dolls managed to find their way home before the Palmers returned. If they didn't, well, Annabelle just couldn't think about that at the moment.

"What about *them*?" asked Tilly May, pointing to Tiffany and Bailey.

"Our clothes are plastic," said Tiffany gaily. "We don't have to worry about mud—or much of anything."

"Nope!" said Bailey, splashing happily through a puddle.

"Uh-oh," said Bobby, a moment later.

"What's the matter?" asked Annabelle, who had just noticed that the clouds had cleared again.

Bobby pointed ahead. "Look where the tracks go."

Annabelle groaned.

The tracks had led the dolls to a stream swollen with rainwater, and instead of turning and following the stream, the tracks simply stopped.

"Jonah and William must have pulled the wagons through the water to the other side," said Bailey.

Annabelle eyed the stream. "Well, we can't follow them."

"Maybe we can," said Bobby thoughtfully.

"No, Annabelle's right," said Tiffany. "We'd get swept away."

"We'd get swept away if we crossed *here* because it's too deep," said Bobby. "The best place to cross a stream is at its widest point. The water's shallower there."

"Wow," said Tiffany.

"Wow," said Tilly.

But Annabelle said, "I'm sorry, Bobby, but I don't think we have time to find the widest point."

"We don't want to turn back," said

Bailey. "We've come such a long way."

Annabelle looked to her left. The stream burbled and gurgled, flowing over rocks and tree branches. She looked to her right and saw the same sight. "I don't know what to do. If we follow the stream, we'll lose the tracks entirely."

"Then we'll have to cross it," said Tiffany. "But how?"

"But how?" echoed Tilly, and Tiffany gave her a dark glance.

"Spread out," said Bobby. "Let's see what we can find."

The dolls walked up and down the bank of the stream, until finally Tiffany called out, "Hey!"

"Hey!" called Tilly May.

Tiffany ignored her. "Bailey and I just

found a place where we can cross the stream without getting wet. The only thing we need is good balance."

Annabelle eyed Tilly, who attempted to step onto a rock, lost her footing, and landed on a bed of moss. "What do you mean?" she asked Tiffany.

"There's a place right over there where a tree fell down and the trunk is lying across the stream. All we have to do is walk along the trunk."

"Oh, no," said Annabelle. "I mean, that's great, Tiffany. It's a good idea. It's just that Tilly isn't—" Annabelle stopped talking when she realized that Tilly was listening to her. She leaned over and whispered in Tiffany's ear, "Tilly isn't very coordinated."

"No kidding," said Tiffany, watching as

Tilly fell again. And she added, "Wow, she's getting awfully dirty. Well, anyway, we'll just have to help her. We'll hold her hands and walk in a line, with Tilly between us."

And that's what the dolls did. When they reached the fallen tree, Bobby scrambled onto it first so he could lead the way. Tiffany followed him, and Bailey and Annabelle handed Tilly up to her. Annabelle climbed up next, and the three girls held hands, Tilly in the middle. Bailey brought up the rear. He was to be on the lookout in case anybody fell in the water.

From the ground, the stream hadn't looked very wide. But when Annabelle stood on the end of the tree trunk, the other bank suddenly seemed miles away, and the water far beneath her.

Tiffany glanced at her friend and said, "Don't look down. Look straight ahead."

The dolls, wobbling slightly, set off for the other side of the stream.

TWENTY
LA

MINUTES
TER

When at last Bobby was poised over dry land, he shouted, "Wah-hoo!" and jumped into a pile of leaves. Moments later the others had joined him, and they lay on their backs, looking at the darkening sky above.

"Oh, dear," said Annabelle finally, eyeing her brother and sister. She sat up. "We didn't get wet, and that's a good thing, but look at the three of us. We're *so* muddy. How on earth are we going to get clean? You guys are pretty dirty too," Annabelle continued, turning to Tiffany and Bailey, "but all you need is a good bath."

"Annabelle, stop worrying about your clothes," said Tiffany. "We'll have nearly two weeks to clean them after we get home. Right now we need to look for the wagon tracks."

"It isn't just our clothes I'm worried about," Annabelle wailed. "It's everything. We have to find the way home, then we have to *get* home, which will take a while. So, Tiffany, we most likely do *not* have two weeks to clean our clothes. There's a good chance, you know, that we might not return before the end of the Palmers' vacation. Even if we do, there's still the issue of . . . of T. M. What about her?"

"Are you saying we shouldn't go home?" asked Bobby.

"No!" exclaimed Annabelle. "Not at all. We *have* to go home."

"All right," said Tiffany, "then we have to find the wagon tracks. So come on, everybody. Focus."

"Focus!" said Tilly May.

"Bobby, you lead the way," said Annabelle.

Bobby set off along the stream. He kept peering at the opposite bank. Finally he said, "If the boys went straight across the stream, they should have come out right about here."

The dolls searched the grass and leaves

and mud, but saw no wagon tracks.

"Maybe they came out farther along," said Bobby. "Up there."

The dolls searched again. Nothing.

They searched up and down the bank for more than an hour, but didn't spot a single track or footprint.

"Finding the wagon tracks was the first step toward going home," said Annabelle dully. "We're not off to a very good start."

"And now it's almost dark," said Bailey.

"I think," said Tiffany, "that we're going to be spending the night in the woods after all."

CHAPTER SEVEN

A Night in the Deep Dark Woods

AT TIFFANY'S WORDS, the dolls turned to Bobby. "Is that right?" asked Annabelle.

Bobby looked apologetic. "Yes. So we'd better get to work building a shelter."

"Why do we need a shelter?" asked Bailey. "We're dolls. We don't sleep."

"I know why we need a shelter," said Annabelle. "It's to hide us, isn't it?"

"If it rains—" Bobby started to say.

But Annabelle rushed on. "I knew it! We have to hide. And there's only one thing we'd need to hide from, and that's animals.

Possums, raccoons, owls, bats—"

"Well, let's not waste time standing around worrying," said Tiffany. "We need to get to work. What should we do, Bobby?"

Bobby frowned. "I think we should try to make a lean-to. We ought to be able to do that pretty quickly."

"What's a lean-to?" asked Annabelle.

"It's a simple structure made from—well, humans would make one from branches or saplings, but those would be too big for us. We'll look for small sticks. What you do is build just half of—" Bobby stopped talking. "I think it's easier to show you what I mean. Everybody go find sticks, okay?"

"But don't wander too far," said Tiffany.

"Maybe we should stay together," said Bobby.

Annabelle had gathered an entire armload of sticks by the time she heard Bobby exclaim, "Hey! Look what I found!"

Annabelle looked. Her brother was tugging at the corner of a plastic bag. "What are you going to do with that?" she asked.

"Make a tent." Bobby continued tugging. "We can make a tent much faster than a lean-to, and plastic is waterproof, which will be good in case it rains tonight. Come on."

Annabelle dropped her sticks, and Bobby pulled the bag to a spot under an oak tree. "This is a good place for our shelter," he announced. "Let's cut the side seams of the bag so we can open it out into one big piece of plastic."

He turned to Bailey. "See if you can do that using the corner of this rock. It looks pretty sharp. Then we'll drape the bag over that low branch and anchor the corners to the ground. The rest of you sharpen some sticks. We'll use them for tent stakes."

"Bobby, this is brilliant!" cried Tiffany when the tent was finished.

Tilly poked her head in one end of the tent, then scrambled back out, exclaiming, "Somefing!"

Annabelle and Tiffany glanced at each other.

"What?" said Annabelle.

Tilly wrinkled her nose.

"I'll go see," said Tiffany. She stepped inside the tent,

then immediately ran back out to the others.

"What is it called?" asked Tilly May, hopping from one foot to the other.

"It's called a very bad smell," replied

Tiffany. "I don't want to complain, but I think this bag once held garbage."

Bobby poked his head in the tent and groaned. "It definitely held something really smelly. I guess we didn't notice it from the outside." He kicked at an acorn.

"It's okay," said Annabelle kindly. "Maybe the smell will fade. Anyway, none of the rest of us could have made a tent like this. I have an idea. Why don't we sit outside the tent? We'll only go in it if we have to hide or if it begins to rain again, okay?"

"Okay," said Bobby and Bailey and Tiffany.

"Very bad smell!" announced Tilly.

"Yes, we know," said Annabelle.

The five dolls sat in a circle among the roots of the tree.

"Well, this is dull," said Tiffany after a while.

"Dull!" cried Annabelle. "It's pitch black, and everywhere I look I think I see animal eyes." She stood up and pointed past the tent. "What's that? What's that?"

Tiffany stood too and peered into the woods. "I don't see a thing."

"I don't see a fing," said Tilly, a small smile on her lips.

"Well, I do," said Annabelle. "Those eyes could belong to a weasel or a groundhog. Or a fisher! Do you know what fishers are?"

"Yes," replied Bobby. "And fishers can be vicious. But I just don't think you're going to find a fisher in the middle of a park, Annabelle."

"What about a snake? Do snakes' eyes shine like other animals'?"

"Annabelle," said Tiffany, "as your aunt would say, 'For the love of Mike, stop it!'"

"For the love of Mike, stop it!" said Tilly.

Tiffany glared at Tilly May. "Tilly," she said, "I feel sorry for you, being in that box and all, but if you don't stop repeating everything I say, you are going to be very, very sorry."

"You are going to be very, very sorry," said Tilly.

Tiffany jumped to her feet. "Tilly, I mean it!"

"Tilly, I mean it!"

"Tilly!"

"Tilly!"

At this moment, Bailey jumped to his feet too, and Annabelle had the horrible thought that he was going to grab Tilly. Instead, he let out a scream, then shouted, "Everybody, into the tent! Right now."

Annabelle turned—and found herself eye to eye with a furry, masked face.

"What it is!" shrieked Tilly, and Annabelle nearly laughed.

"Raccoon!" cried Tiffany, just as the raccoon opened its mouth.

Annabelle couldn't move. She felt as if she might be in Doll State. She watched Bobby hoist Tilly to his hip, watched the others run for cover, and still she felt leaden. Finally Bobby thrust his hand out one end of the tent and hauled Annabelle inside. "All right," he said, gasping. "Be quiet, all of you. Don't move, don't speak."

Annabelle sat on the ground, breathing heavily and trying to ignore the odor of the plastic bag. She listened closely and could hear the pattering of the raccoon's paws outside the little tent. Annabelle recalled something about raccoons liking to raid garbage cans. If that was true, and if the tent did indeed smell like garbage, then this was not good, not good at all.

Annabelle reached for Tilly, pulled her sister into her lap, and told herself not to panic. Calm, calm, calm. She didn't know how long the raccoon sniffed and snuffled around the tent, but it seemed like hours. Nobody spoke. Even Tilly May sat silently in the darkness.

Annabelle quietly shifted her
position and rearranged Tilly.
She made herself think of cozy
nights in the Dolls' house:
nights spent posed in the nursery
while on the other side of Kate's
room, Grandma Katherine perched on the
edge of her granddaughter's bed, and she and
Kate took turns reading aloud to each other.
On one of those nights, Kate had yawned,
closed the book they were reading, and said
sleepily, "Have you ever gone camping?"

"No indeed," Grandma Katherine had
replied. "But I know plenty of people who
love spending the night in fresh air, getting
away from the comforts and conveniences of
civilized life. They like hearing crickets chirping and owls hooting and the little sounds of
nighttime creatures running by their tent."

"Mmm. Maybe we could go camping
sometime," Kate had said.

And Annabelle had felt a longing
for adventure.

But now she thought, Never again! I will
never, ever, ever go camping again.

The moon had risen, been briefly obscured
by a cloud, then slid across the sky before the
dolls felt safe enough to speak. Annabelle was
just thinking about peeping around one end
of the smelly tent when from out of the darkness sounded a high-pitched: *WAUGHHHHHHH!*

Annabelle let out a shriek of her own,
then clapped her hand over her mouth and
tried to hug Tilly and Tiffany at the same time.
"What was that?" she managed to whisper.

Tiffany was speechless. So was Bailey. He

merely shook his head. Bobby replied, voice low, "It sounded human."

Annabelle glanced down at her little sister. "Try not to be scared," she said.

But Tilly looked up at her and smiled. "Barn owl," she announced. "Adult call."

"What?" said Annabelle and the others.

"I fink it's a barn owl."

Tilly paused, and the screech came again: *WAUGHHHHHHH!*

"Yes," said Tilly May. "Adult barn owl."

"How do you know that?" asked Tiffany. "From another tape?"

Tilly nodded. "Owls Around the World— call number firteen."

"What's a barn owl doing in the middle of a town park?" asked Bailey.

Bobby shrugged. "Maybe it's lost, like we are. The important thing about barn owls, though, is that they hunt by sound only. So if the owl doesn't hear us, it won't come after us."

The dolls huddled silently in the tent. They waited for what Annabelle guessed was more than an hour.

At last Bailey said, to no one in particular, "Do you think they're gone? Both of them?"

Bobby replied, "I don't know about the owl, but I think the raccoon would have come in the tent by now, if it were going to."

It was Tiffany who finally worked up the courage to get to her feet and peer around one end of the tent. Then she glanced back over her shoulder and said importantly, "I don't see anything, and I don't hear anything. But I think we should stay inside the tent for the rest of the night. It'll be safer. Tomorrow, when there's enough light to see by, we can leave."

"Okay," said Bobby. "I was thinking the same thing. And you know what else? I was thinking about the fact that we *are* in a park. That means that we can't really get lost here. If we just pick one direction and walk in it, eventually we'll walk out of the park. There's no way to know which direction will get us out of the park the fastest, but we can't help that."

"How will we know if we get off course?" asked Bailey.

"We'll follow the sun," replied Bobby.

The dolls waited patiently and quietly until the first light of morning. Then they stepped out of the tent (Annabelle realized that she hardly noticed the smell now), and Bobby looked all around. "I think we should go east," he said.

"Then that's what we'll do," said Tiffany.

"Then that's—" Tilly May started to say, but she stopped herself. She put her hand in Annabelle's, and the dolls set off.

They walked on as straight a course as they could manage. Sometimes they had to go out of their way—to walk around a rock or a tree or to find a place where they could cross a stream. Then they looked for the sun again and continued east.

The sun was almost directly over their heads when Annabelle heard a sound that wasn't leaves rustling or an animal scurrying or a birdcall.

"Stop," said Annabelle. "I hear . . . I think I hear a car."

The dolls stood still, and Annabelle noticed that ahead of them was a stone wall.

"I hear it too," said Bailey. "I hear lots of cars."

"Traffic," said Bobby. "This must be the edge of the park."

"Bobby, you did it!" exclaimed Annabelle.

Bobby grinned.

The dolls made their way to the wall and walked beside it until they came to a gap in the stones. They peered around the wall. A busy street lay before them.

"We're downtown again," said Tiffany. "Now what do we do?"

CHAPTER EIGHT

Dollies for Sale

ANNABELLE DREW BACK behind the wall. "We have to leave the park," she said. "But how are we going to stay hidden out there?" Her voice rose to a squeak.

"Don't panic," said Tiffany. She peeked through the opening again at the sidewalk beyond. "Well, there's bad news and good news," she reported, "and they're both the same. The bad news is that there are about a billion people over there. But that's the good news too, because it's so busy, I don't think anyone will notice us. So just follow me and try not to get trampled."

"But where are we going?" asked Annabelle.

Tiffany drew in a deep breath. "I don't have all the answers right now. Let's just get going and I'll think of something."

The dolls followed Tiffany to the sidewalk and turned right. Annabelle looked ahead and saw that the wall ran beside her as far as an intersection, and then ended. Across the intersection was a row of buildings that Annabelle thought were probably stores.

Holding tightly to Tilly's hand, Annabelle set bravely forth, but had taken no more than two steps when a shadow passed over her and she came within inches of being crushed by a shoe. Annabelle gasped and whisked Tilly out of the way, nearly smashing her against the wall in her haste. She turned around in time to see Bobby dodge a sandal and Bailey run from the path of a baby carriage.

"This is crazy!" exclaimed Bobby.

Everywhere the dolls looked were feet or wheels.

"What's that?" asked Tilly.

"Pigeon!" shrieked Annabelle.

Just then, Tiffany cried, "Oh, yuck! Gum!"

"Stay away from the gum!" cried Annabelle, and she yanked at Tilly again.

"You know what?" said Tiffany. "I think we need to cross that street and go inside one of those stores. It's too dangerous to stay out here."

"How are we going to cross the street?" asked Bobby.

"I know," said Bailey. "See that stroller? The one that's moving slowly? As fast as you can, run to it and jump onto the shelf on the bottom. We'll hitch a ride to the nearest store."

Annabelle, praying that the stroller would cross the street, ran toward the little shelf, Tilly in tow, and hopped aboard. The dolls landed in a heap.

"Have we reached the street yet?" asked Annabelle when the stroller came to a stop.

Bobby crept to the edge of the shelf and looked around. "We're about to cross it right now," he reported. "And I think there's a huge store on the corner. So when I say 'Go,' everyone jump off, okay?"

"Okay," whispered the dolls.

"Go!" cried Bobby a few moments later, and the dolls scrambled onto the sidewalk again.

"Is this the store?" asked Tiffany.

The dolls were standing in front of a giant revolving door. Written across the glass, far above their heads, was one word. Annabelle tipped her head back to read it:

"This must be the department store where the Palmers sometimes shop," she said. "And look. There's a door that turns around and around."

"Well, hurry up. Let's go," said Tiffany as she narrowly escaped being lapped up by a red tongue belonging to a very hairy white dog.

The dolls ran toward the revolving door, Annabelle clutching Tilly and murmuring, "Oh, no, oh, no, oh, no." Before she knew it she had been swept along by a small brush on the bottom of the door, which shot her into the store.

"Hide!" said Bailey in a loud whisper.

The dolls streaked toward the nearest wall and hid between it and a shoe box. For several moments, no one spoke.

Finally Bailey (sounding faintly annoyed) said, "What are we going to do *now*?"

Annabelle squared her shoulders. "We need another plan."

"I think we should hide somewhere until the store isn't so crowded," said Bobby.

"Yes," agreed Tiffany, gazing around. After a moment, she said, "It's hard to see much from here. It's just an ocean of feet."

"Someone should climb up on something and look down from above," said Bobby.

"That's a good idea," said Annabelle. "But I think that whatever we do, we should do together. Nobody should go off alone. It's too easy to get separated," she added, shuddering slightly as a shopping bag was banged down nearby, and a broom swept past the little dolls. "My goodness, this is a busy place," she said. "Almost as busy as the street."

"Well, we're not going back out there," said Tiffany.

"No, no," replied Annabelle hurriedly. "I didn't mean that. Okay. Where should we go for a look around the store? It has to be someplace we can all get to."

It was Bobby who realized that they could climb to the top of a nearby display counter in a messy corner of the store. "See? We can pull ourselves onto that box, and from the box onto that carton, and then up those little holes that hold the shelves in place. We can use them like a ladder."

This all took much more effort than the dolls had imagined, especially for Tilly, who was shorter than the others and also not used to so much exercise. But in the end, Annabelle, Tiffany, Bailey, Bobby, and Tilly May huffed and puffed their way onto the glass countertop and sat down in a row near the edge.

"Try not to move too much," said Annabelle, speaking out of the corner of her mouth. "We do *not* want to go into Doll State here. It would be a disaster."

"What's a disaster?" asked Tilly.

Annabelle sighed. "I'll have to explain later. Just do what we do. Pretend you're a statue. It's a fun game."

"What's a statue?" asked Tilly.

"Something that doesn't move, and most important," said Tiffany, "*doesn't speak.* So *Shh.*"

Annabelle slid her eyes slightly to the left and looked down the length of the counter. It was filled with racks of earrings and necklaces and bracelets. "This is a jewelry counter," she whispered to Tiffany, barely moving her lips. "Costume jewelry, I guess." Then she looked ahead at the rest of the store, which spread out in front of her the way the first floor of the Palmers' house did when Annabelle stood at the top of the staircase.

"I think—" Annabelle was saying, when suddenly a woman wearing a businesslike suit and a name tag reading MS. LEWIS swooped in front of the counter. Annabelle could only pray that Tilly would hold still and keep quiet.

"Well, my word," said Ms. Lewis, and she clicked her tongue disapprovingly. "How did these dolls get here? They belong in the toy department. Honestly, this store looks more and more like a jumble sale every day. If Mr. McGinitie could see it, he'd roll over in his grave. Shoes in Housewares, dolls in Jewelry . . ."

Annabelle had rarely heard anyone speak her thoughts out loud at such length, and personally felt that perhaps they ought to be kept in one's head. She became so fascinated by Ms. Lewis and her thoughts, though, that she momentarily forgot about the trouble she was in, and so she was shocked when Ms. Lewis placed her hand on the counter and in one motion, swept the five dolls over the edge and into the pocket of her jacket. "Upstairs to Toys for you," she said firmly.

And just like that, Annabelle found herself in the middle of a doll sandwich in Ms. Lewis's pocket, which also contained a safety pin, two folded pieces of paper, a dime, a cough drop, and a used Kleenex.

"Keep *away* from the Kleenex," Annabelle hissed to Tilly. "Seriously."

"What is—" Tilly started to ask, but Annabelle poked her. "Shh."

Bobby and Tiffany were underneath Annabelle in the pocket, and Tilly and Bailey were above her. Bailey's shoe was in her face, and something was resting heavily on her head. Annabelle inched away from the shoe, but as soon as she moved, she felt Ms. Lewis clamp her hand on the pocket. At this, Tilly let out a squeak, so Annabelle clamped her own hand over Tilly's mouth, and in this way, the five dolls made the rest of their journey up the escalator to the second floor of McGinitie's.

After much jostling, the world of the pocket grew still. Annabelle dared to remove her hand from Tilly's mouth. The dolls waited. A few moments later they heard Ms. Lewis say, "Nell? Nell? Come over here, please." And after a pause, "Just look at what I found downstairs in Jewelry." Ms. Lewis's hand reached into the pocket and, one by one, withdrew the dolls and placed them in a row on what Annabelle assumed was another counter; but since Ms. Lewis had placed the dolls on their backs, all Annabelle could see was the ceiling. Then Ms. Lewis's face loomed above her, joined by another face, this one more kindly than Ms. Lewis's, which was on the pinched side.

"You found these dolls in Jewelry?" asked the kind face.

Ms. Lewis was huffy. "Yes. These two dirty plastic ones, and these beautiful antique ones."

Beautiful? Annabelle felt somewhat relieved at the word. Perhaps she and Bobby and Tilly didn't look as messy as she feared they did.

Nell squinted down at the dolls. "Well," she said, "the Funcraft dolls obviously came from the play area. They can go right back there. But the antique dolls . . . I suppose they must have come in from an estate sale, although how they wound up downstairs is a mystery. But if they just arrived, well, that would explain their condition." She clucked her tongue. "They need to be cleaned up." She turned to Ms. Lewis. "Don't worry. I'll take care of everything."

"All right," said Ms. Lewis, who left without saying thank you.

Nell regarded the dolls. "First things first," she said lightly. "Back to the play area for these two." She whisked Tiffany and Bailey off the counter, disappeared, and returned a few moments later without them. "Now for the older dolls," she murmured.

Nell gently picked up Annabelle, Bobby, and Tilly, and wound her way through the store to an unmarked door. She opened the door, bustled inside, and laid the Dolls on a counter next to a sink. She considered them for a few moments, then carefully removed their stained clothing. (Tilly held admirably still.) Nell left with the clothing (tsking at its condition), and when she returned she said

cheerfully, "Okay, bath time!" And she knew just how to bathe the dolls, which were made partly of easy-to-clean porcelain and partly of hard-to-clean cloth. Later she brought their clothing back, now bright and stain-free, if a little damp.

Nell dressed the Dolls, held Annabelle aloft for close inspection, set her down again, bustled about, and finally laid Annabelle,

Tilly, and Bobby in a box lined with tissue paper. "Off we go," she said.

The ceiling bumping along above her, Annabelle and her sister and brother were returned to the toy department. Annabelle listened carefully for sounds from outside the box. She heard voices and clatters and footsteps, and then the box came to rest and the ceiling stopped moving.

"All right. Into the case," said Nell.

Annabelle was lifted from the box and saw ahead of her a wide glass display case holding rows of dolls of varying sizes, all perched on metal stands. Most of the dolls appeared to be either antique, like the Dolls, or fancy and expensive. But, thought Annabelle, they weren't very neatly arranged. In fact, they had been placed haphazardly, and here and there Annabelle glimpsed empty stands.

Nell's hand reached out and opened the case, and Annabelle was placed inside on a shelf. Moments later, Bobby was placed on her left and Tilly May on Bobby's left. Each was propped up on one of the stands, feet not quite touching the shelf, and there they remained in a stiff row for the duration of the afternoon.

Annabelle was tempted to panic but chose instead to study the toy department. She had a good view of it, and felt it might be wise to become familiar with her new surroundings. Also, she hoped to catch a glimpse of Tiffany and Bailey. Nell had taken them to the play area, Annabelle remembered. Play area. Now where could that be? Annabelle turned her head a fraction of an inch so she could see better. Everywhere she looked were shelves stocked from floor to ceiling with dolls (Annabelle wondered how many of them might be live dolls) and toys— games and puzzles and Barbies and trucks and skateboards and fire engines and baby dolls

and trains and craft sets and talking dolls and magic kits and building blocks and doll clothes. Amazing. Fascinating. But what had Nell meant by the play area?

Then Annabelle noticed two girls seated at a plastic table, vigorously zooming wooden cars back and forth across a decidedly scuffed surface. On the floor at their feet, a boy was linking train tracks into a loop. He reached under the table, pulled out a battered dump truck, and set it on the track.

In the back of the truck were Tiffany and Bailey.

Oh, thought Annabelle. The play area. It was full of old toys—toys that were too old to sell—and it was a place in which children could play while their parents shopped. Annabelle felt sorry for Tiffany and Bailey, deemed worthy only of the play area. Then she looked at the display case—at her glass cage—and at the other dolls on her shelf. That was when she noticed a price tag assigned to each doll. Annabelle drew in her breath. Price tags. The dolls in this case were for sale. Of course they were. How long until she and Bobby and Tilly were given price tags as well?

* * *

The day slid away from Annabelle. She sat on her perch and thought of her family safe in their home. She thought of her other little sister, who must miss Annabelle and Bobby. Beside her, Tilly May remained remarkably still, and Annabelle felt proud of her. The crowds thinned, the toy department grew quiet. Through a faraway window Annabelle watched the sky become gray. At last she heard a tinny voice announce, "Attention, all shoppers. McGinitie's will close in fifteen minutes. Please pay for your purchases and exit the store. Thank you."

When fifteen minutes had passed, the last of the shoppers left the toy department and glided out of sight down the escalator. Silence. Annabelle was thinking how long the night was going to seem, when she heard a clank, then another clank, then a bang, and then voices. Presently two men and a woman lugging mops, buckets, and vacuum cleaners appeared from around a corner. One of them— a lanky man with a mustache—disappeared, then reappeared pushing a cart full of cleaning supplies. The three worked quietly, returning toys to shelves or to the play area, mopping the aisles, vacuuming the carpet, dusting the countertops.

The man with the mustache seemed to be in charge, and every now and then one of the others would say to him, "Charlie, we're almost out of Windex." Or, "There was a sale in Shoes today. I bet that department's going to be a mess." Charlie would nod and make a note on a pad of paper, then continue tidying the toy department, pausing to straighten a stack of puzzles or replace a doll's shoe. Annabelle watched as he rebuilt part of the LEGO display, and then reattached a leg to a Funcraft doll that looked alarmingly like Bailey. At last Charlie took a final look around, paying careful attention to the play area. He nodded with satisfaction. "Okay," he said. "I think we're done here. Come on."

The lights dimmed, and the toy department grew silent. Annabelle watched a clock on the wall. After half an hour she noticed a buzz of excitement in the air. It was all around her. She was just wondering whether it was safe to move, when a voice from within the display case said, "Party time!"

CHAPTER NINE

Nighttime in McGinitie's

ANNABELLE LOOKED around the toy department in wonder. Doll by doll, it began to come to life. She watched in fascination as dolls of all kinds and sizes jumped off shelves, slid off tables, and climbed down from displays. A very large doll—Annabelle thought she must be at least three feet tall—opened the glass case and began to lift out the antique and fancy dolls, setting them gently on the floor.

"Hello!" she said in a friendly voice when she reached Annabelle, Bobby, and Tilly. "You three are new. Are you antique or just expensive? You look antique," she continued, before Annabelle could answer her. "Where are you from? An estate sale? That's where we get most of the antique dolls from. I'm Marisol, by the way. Here. Let me get you down. Gosh, you guys are little."

"Hey!" exclaimed Bobby. "We are not little."

"Yes, you are. Compared to me, anyway," said Marisol cheerfully. "Most everyone is. But it doesn't matter." She placed the Dolls on the floor. "Go on and introduce your-selves. Have fun. I have to let the others out."

Marisol continued to empty the glass case, then moved to the shelves and began to lift down a row of baby dolls in their boxes, their excited faces peeking out through cello-phane. Annabelle noticed that Marisol did not, however, open the boxes.

"Annabelle!" called Bobby. "Come on, there's a picnic!"

Annabelle, holding Tilly's hand as usual, turned her attention to the wide aisle through the toy department. Dozens and dozens of live dolls were setting out miniature lawn chairs and fake food, blankets and grills, beach balls and croquet sets. Where, she wondered, had all these items come from, and how would the dolls get them back in place before the store opened in the morning?

Everywhere she looked, dolls were playing and laughing and running and calling to one another.

"We have to find Tiffany and Bailey," said Annabelle to her brother.

But Bobby's reply was, "Look, baseball! I always wanted

to play baseball. I'm going over there. See you later." And just like that he disappeared into the crowd of happy dolls.

"Bobby!" Annabelle called. "Be careful! Remember how easily you crack."

"Don't worry about him," said a silky voice, and Annabelle turned to find a flat plastic doll, taller than Annabelle by several inches, standing at her elbow. The doll was dressed in an outfit similar to the one Nora Palmer wore to her gymnastics classes. "He'll be okay," said the doll. "Really. The others will watch out for him."

Annabelle looked at the doll's friendly face, her

black pants, her purple top, and matching purple headband, and noticed that she was barefoot. "Have you—have you lived here a long time?" she asked.

"Well, most of us don't actually *live* here," replied the doll. "As you can imagine. This is just a sort of way station. We only stay here until we're sold and can live with a human of our own in a home of our own. I've been here for about two weeks. I'm lucky to be a display doll. The rest of my kind"—she gestured over her shoulder to a row of similar dolls packaged neatly in cardboard boxes— "are Shut-ins."

"What are Shut-ins?" asked Annabelle.

"The ones stuck in the boxes. They can see us and hear us, but we can't let them out.

We'd never get them all fastened properly into the boxes again by morning. They're held in place with twist ties and tape and cardboard and Styrofoam."

Annabelle looked at the rows of faces peering out through cellophane. Marisol had set some of their boxes on the floor next to the baby dolls, so that they could be closer to the fun; but still, the boxes were shut tight.

Annabelle shivered. Then she turned back to the doll in the gymnastics outfit. "So you're on display," she said, "and you don't have a box. Will you still be sold?"

"Eventually. I don't get played with during the day—not like the dolls in the play area. I just get looked at. So I stay in good condition. Someone will buy me after the ones in the boxes have sold. Or else I'll get marked down. There's my display," she added, pointing to a shelf near the checkout counter. "See? I come with a yoga mat, a silk eye mask, and a

152

bottle of min-
eral water. Well,
not real water, of
course, just a bottle with a
label that says 'Mineral Water.'"
The doll patted her ponytail.
"So," she said. "What's your
name?"

"I'm Annabelle Doll,"
said Annabelle. "And this is
my little sister Tilly May."

"I'm Elsipad. I
named myself. I'll get a
new name as soon as
someone buys
me," she added.
Annabelle
had a long

list of questions she wanted to ask Elsipad about McGinitie's and the toy department, but instead she said, "When we got here today we were with two other dolls, and someone took them to the play area. I saw them earlier, but now I don't know where they are. Have you seen any Funcraft dolls?"

Elsipad laughed. "*Any* Funcraft dolls?! There are only about a million of them here. They're some of the most popular dolls in the store. Which ones are you looking for?"

"Tiffany and Bailey."

"Wow," said Elsipad. "And Tiffany and Bailey are the most popular Funcrafts. There are probably a couple hundred of each of them here. And they all look exactly alike."

"Two hundred?" cried Annabelle. "Of *each* of them?"

Elsipad nodded. "See those buckets over there? During the day they're filled with Tiffanys and Baileys. And more Tiffanys and Baileys are included in the sets that come with houses and furniture and stuff."

"But how am I going to tell *my* Tiffany and Bailey apart from the others?" asked Annabelle uneasily.

"Don't worry," replied Elsipad calmly. "*They'll* be able to find *you*. You don't look like anyone else here."

"That's true, I guess," said Annabelle, conscious of her green hair. But she was envisioning her worries in a growing pile that was in danger of toppling over. Now she wasn't even certain she had seen Tiffany and Bailey in the dump truck. Not her Tiffany and Bailey, anyway.

"If you don't mind my asking," said Elsipad, "how did you happen to come in here today with two *old* Funcraft dolls? All the dolls in McGinitie's come directly from the factory, except for the antique ones. We never get dolls that go straight to the play area."

Annabelle sighed. "Actually, we're not supposed to be here. It's a long story."

"I love long stories. Will you tell me yours?" Elsipad took Annabelle by the hand and led her to a Funcraft-size plastic couch, Tilly trailing behind them. "We can sit here where it's quiet. Tell me everything."

So Annabelle did. She told Elsipad about finding Tilly May and about running away, about spending the night in the woods with the raccoon and the owl nearby, about making their way to McGinitie's, and finally about Ms. Lewis and Nell. "Nell cleaned us up," Annabelle reported, "and brought us back here, but she'd already taken Tiffany and Bailey to the play area."

Elsipad raised her eyebrows. "That's an amazing story!"

"Yes," said Annabelle. "And you see why we have to find Tiffany and Bailey. We have to

figure out some way to get home."

"Finding Tiffany and Bailey is going to be the easy part," said Elsipad.

Annabelle nodded.

"Don't look so worried." Elsipad smiled. "I come with a motto. It's printed on the front of my box. Guess what the motto is."

Annabelle looked thoughtful. Then she shook her head.

"Can *you* guess?" Elsipad asked Tilly.

Tilly, who had been sitting quietly, stacking a set of teeny alphabet blocks, said, "What's a motto?"

"Words to live by," replied Elsipad. "I think."

"Don't know," said Tilly.

"My motto," said Elsipad proudly, "is 'Don't worry, be happy.'"

"Tiffany would like that motto," said Annabelle.

"Well, look. Like I said, Tiffany will be able to find you, so try to stop worrying. Think about something else."

Annabelle forced a smile. "Tell me *your* story," she said.

"Mine isn't quite as interesting

as yours," replied Elsipad, "but okay. I came from a factory, the Best Toys factory in New Jersey. I was completed on a Thursday, and that night I took the oath, along with all the other dolls who were ready to be shipped out. I arrived at McGinitie's two weeks ago, and that's my story. I can't wait to be adopted by my Forever Girl or Forever Boy and have a true home, a home of my own—but I know that might take a while. Oh! Guess what else it says on my box." Elsipad closed her eyes and quoted, "'A portion of the proceeds of the sale of this product will be used to fight world hunger.' Isn't that wonderful?"

Annabelle was impressed. And she was about to say so when she heard a familiar voice call, "Annabelle! Annabelle Doll!"

Annabelle jumped to her feet. A bright red pickup truck decorated with glittery peace signs was zooming toward the couch, and in the back of the truck was Tiffany, waving her arms.

"Tiffany! Is it

really you?" asked Annabelle, as the truck carrying her friend (she sincerely hoped this doll was in fact her old friend Tiffany) jerked to a stop.

"Yes! It's really me!" Tiffany leaped out of the truck, and she and Annabelle threw their arms around each other.

"You know how many of you are here, don't you?" asked Annabelle.

"I have a pretty good idea. Dakota Jane was telling me about all the Funcrafts, and I've already seen a lot of Tiffanys. That's Dakota Jane," added Tiffany, and she pointed to the driver of the truck, who now stepped out and greeted Elsipad.

Dakota Jane (another display doll, Annabelle learned) came with the truck, and wore a long denim skirt, a belt with a rhinestone buckle, and a blue cowgirl hat and cowgirl boots. She and Elsipad had become best friends.

"DJ's truck really runs," said Tiffany, who sounded awfully impressed.

"Well, not on gas," said DJ. "You wind it up, then hop in—fast—and away you go. I just steer the truck until it winds down. Want to take a ride?"

"Yes! Yes!" exclaimed Tilly May, springing to life. She scrambled to her feet, sending the blocks flying.

"Well, come on then," said DJ. "Elsipad and I will introduce you to our friends."

Annabelle, Tiffany, and Tilly climbed
into the back of the truck, along with Elsipad,
who called to Dakota Jane, "Don't wind it up
too much. Let's just go for a nice slow ride."

So the truck inched along the aisle of the
toy department, something Annabelle
thought Baby Betsy might enjoy quite a bit,
and every so often Elsipad would see another
of their friends. "There's Rose-up," she said
as they passed a small cloth doll sitting on a

blanket. "She's a baby. We all take turns looking after the baby dolls, especially the ones
who aren't in boxes." The truck moved on.
"Oh, there's Dr. Sue!" cried Elsipad. "She's a
vet. She comes with animals—just plastic
ones—and a doctor's kit with real bandages in

it." Elsipad waved to Dr. Sue, who waved back.
"And there are the twins," continued Elsipad,
pointing to two of the strangest dolls
Annabelle had ever seen. "They call themselves
Vixamax McBeevay and Viramax McGeehan."

"Why don't they have the same last name?" asked Tiffany.

Elsipad shrugged. "Who knows? Maybe because they aren't identical twins."

"That doesn't make—" Tiffany started to say, but Annabelle interrupted her. "What . . . what *are* they?" she stammered.

"What do you mean?" asked Elsipad.

"Well, Vixamax and Viramax—are they really dolls? One of them's plugged into a socket, as if he were a vacuum cleaner or a blender."

"They're really dolls," replied Elsipad, just as Dakota Jane called from the front of the truck. "They're hybrids! They're a cross between a doll and a DTD. And Vixamax isn't plugged into a socket. He's plugged into his docking station. You can play with the hybrids online *and* offline. That's why we call them the On-Offs," she added.

Annabelle felt more confused than ever. "I have absolutely no idea what you're talking about," she said. She turned to Tiffany. "Do you?"

Tiffany nodded solemnly. "Yes," she replied. "DTD stands for *Data Transfer Device*."

"And what is a *data transfer device*?" asked Annabelle, beginning to feel quite cross.

"It's like an iPod."

"Viramax and Vixamax are part of the American iDoll Collection," DJ shouted gaily from the driver's seat.

"You see," said Tiffany patiently, "the twins are display dolls, and I was watching kids play with them this afternoon. You can play with the iDolls like regular dolls—"

"But how?" Annabelle interrupted. "Viramax and Vixamax don't look like they can move at all. Their feet are fused together to make that plug thing. And they have a cord coming out of their heads."

"Or," Tiffany rushed on, "you can plug them into the docking station to unlock computer games and do virtual shopping and stuff."

"What?" said Annabelle.

"Consumer exploitation," muttered Elsipad.

"You can play with Vixamax and Viramax on the computer," Tiffany explained as Vixamax unplugged himself from the docking station. "I mean, with images of them in computer games."

"Then what do you need the real dolls for?" asked Annabelle.

"I already told you. To unlock the computer games. Plus," said Tiffany with great excitement, "do you see how each of the dolls has a little computer screen on his stomach? You can download the games into the dolls and play right *on* the American iDolls."

Annabelle just stared. At last she said, "You mean the twins can watch themselves on their own stomachs?"

This time no one answered her, and Annabelle thought that this must be what Tilly May felt like as she asked question after question, trying to understand her new world outside the box.

Moments later, the truck slowed to a stop. Dakota Jane stepped out and said, "Shall I wind it up again?"

Annabelle, attempting to put the On-Offs out of her mind, looked down the aisle of the store. "Is that the baseball game over there?" she asked.

"Yup," said DJ. "I think that's where the twins are headed now."

"Then let's get out here," said Annabelle. "I want to find my brother. Tiffany, is Bailey with Bobby?"

"I think so." Tiffany squinted into the distance. "I see an awful lot of Baileys, though."

Elsipad helped Annabelle and Tilly out of the truck, and they made their way through the crowd of dolls to the baseball game. It was difficult to tell who was playing and who was just watching (since the players weren't wearing uniforms), but of the dolls Annabelle was fairly certain were actually on teams, she counted eight Bailey Funcrafts. She turned to Tiffany in alarm. "How do you know which one is really Bailey?" she asked.

"Excuse me?" said Tiffany.

"How do you know which one is your brother?"

Tiffany turned expressionless eyes on

Annabelle. "I don't understand your question," she said, staring. She cocked her head. "Who are you anyway?"

"I'm Annabelle!" said Annabelle.

Tiffany frowned. "Are you new here?"

"Hey, Annabelle!" A hand tugged at the back of Annabelle's dress. "Sorry we got separated. It's so crowded here."

Annabelle turned around and looked into the face of another Tiffany. Tiffany in front of her, Tiffany behind her. And watching the baseball game, three more Tiffanys. She suppressed a scream.

"Annabelle, it's me. I mean, it's *really* me," said the Tiffany who had tugged at her dress. When Annabelle, mouth open, didn't reply, Tiffany recited, "We live with the Palmers. I belong to Nora, you belong to Kate. The cat's name is The Captain. The grandmother is—"

"Okay, okay. I know it's you," said Annabelle. "But this is weird. Scary weird."

"Yes," agreed Tiffany, suddenly serious. "It is. Maybe I should do something to myself—like put a mark on my face—so you can tell who I am."

"No. You can't go back to the Palmers' with a mark on your face."

"I'll use crayon," said Tiffany. "We can wipe it off before we get home. I'll mark Bailey too. As soon as I find a crayon. Now come on. We'll worry about this later. Let's watch the game. Look, Bobby's at bat."

"He'll never hit the ball," said Annabelle, and at that moment, Bobby's bat connected with the tiny baseball and sent it flying into a shelf full of skateboards.

"Wah-hoo!" shouted Tiffany. "Way to go, Bobby!"

Annabelle watched Viramax and Vixamax hop awkwardly after the ball, their cords

trailing behind them.

"Batter up! Batter up!" Viramax kept calling.

The twins reached the ball. "Here it is!" shouted Vixamax. "Come and get it! Repeat! Somebody who has movable arms, come and get the ball!"

"On my way!" said one of the Bailey Funcrafts.

"Batter up! Batter up!" cried Viramax again.

Annabelle glanced at DJ.

"There's a bit of a glitch in Viramax's system," DJ explained. "A baseball game was downloaded into his stomach, and, well, I

guess something got stuck somewhere. That's all he seems to be able to say."

The Bailey doll emerged from among the skateboards holding the ball aloft, and the game continued.

Annabelle, Tilly, Tiffany, Elsipad, and DJ pushed through the crowd to a quiet area behind the outfield and watched the rest of the game. This was fun, Annabelle admitted. It was fun to be with so many dolls, to make new doll friends, to be free to talk and play. She wished Baby Betsy were here with her. Her little sister—her other little sister—would have enjoyed the excitement.

Annabelle sat with her new friends until the sun came up. As the first rays crept along the walls, the dolls, hurrying, began to put their things away, and then to put themselves away. Marisol picked up Annabelle, Bobby, and Tilly and carried them to the glass case.

"See you tonight!" Elsipad called after them.

Moments later, Marisol had closed the case, and Annabelle, hanging on her stand, feet not quite touching the shelf below, began to think once more of home. And she realized that she and her brother and sister and friends had been away for two nights. By now their parents would be frantic. And there was not a single thing Annabelle could do about that.

CHAPTER TEN

A Strange Disappearance

ANNABELLE, worries mounting, watched as Marisol and the other larger dolls continued their tidying up. Then she searched the toy department for Tiffany (*her* Tiffany) and spotted her in the play area. She knew it was her Tiffany because the Funcraft doll waved to Annabelle and then held a red crayon aloft. When Annabelle waved back, Tiffany aimed the crayon at her face and drew a wobbly T on her plastic forehead. Then she motioned to Bailey and made a B on his forehead.

Annabelle thought this over. At the

Palmers' house, crayon marks on foreheads might have been cause for Doll State. But in the play area of a department store, nobody kept strict track of the dolls and toys, and the store workers wouldn't be alarmed by a change in the appearance of a doll. As long as Tiffany and Bailey were able to wipe the marks off later, they should be okay. Probably.

Annabelle watched Tiffany help Rose-up, the baby, arrange herself on her display blanket, and thought again of Betsy, her giant baby sister, whom she loved dearly, no matter what her size. She wondered what Betsy was doing at that exact moment. Then Annabelle watched Tiffany wave good-bye to Dakota Jane and Elsipad as they drove off in the truck. She was still watching Tiffany when a Mom Funcraft doll appeared and motioned to Tiffany to follow her. Tiffany shook her head and said something, which Annabelle guessed was, "But I'm supposed to stay here in the play area."

The Mom Funcraft doll motioned again, Tiffany shook her head again, and then the mom marched across the tile floor, took Tiffany by the elbow, pulled her down the aisle to a Funcraft Dream House display, and shoved her through the front door. That was the last Annabelle saw of her friend until the evening.

"Bobby!" exclaimed Annabelle. "Did you see what just happened?"

Her brother nodded. "Why do you think she took Tiffany?"

"I don't know. But I met another Tiffany last night, and she was very strange. That mom looked kind of strange too. And did you see that big black mark down her back?"

"The Funcrafts mean well," said a soft voice, and Annabelle jumped.

"Sorry. I didn't mean to scare you." The doll hanging on the stand to Annabelle's right spoke kindly, but turned a stern face to her. "I'm Angelica," she said. "I didn't have a chance to introduce myself to you before."

"I'm Annabelle," said Annabelle timidly, her eyes fixed on Angelica's pursed lips.

"Don't be afraid of me."

"I'm not afraid," Annabelle lied.

"Yes you are. I can tell. And don't worry. Most people are afraid of me. It's my smile," said Angelica ruefully.

"Your smile?" Annabelle saw no smile whatsoever.

"All right, my missing smile. It wore off years ago. I'm old, you know," said Angelica. "Maybe older than you are."

Annabelle studied Angelica, a china doll slightly larger than Elsipad, with wavy black hair and brown eyes, wearing a faded cotton dress. The lace at the collar had once been white, Annabelle supposed, but had long ago turned the color of weak tea. When Annabelle stared at Angelica's mouth she could see that the molded lips indeed turned up in a smile, but that the pink paint had worn off at each end, leaving Angelica with a severe expression.

"We," said Annabelle, "I mean, my brother and sister and I" (here she paused to introduce Angelica to Bobby and Tilly May) "were made in 1898 by a doll maker in London."

"I was made in 1890," said Angelica, "but in New York City."

"How did you get here?" Annabelle wanted to know. "How did you wind up in McGinitie's after all this time?"

Angelica sighed. "I suppose every old doll has a story. I lived with many families and was loved by lots of little girls, first in New York, where I was sold from a toy shop, then in other cities. I even lived in California for several years."

"California!" exclaimed Bobby from his stand.

"Yes," said Angelica. "In the city of San Francisco. Then the family moved to Connecticut, and I've been here ever since, with one family or another. But I haven't belonged to a human in a very long time. In fact, I'd been stuck in a box for ages, in an attic, I think, and then one day I heard voices and I felt the box rise up, and the next thing I knew, I was being unpacked here at the store, and Nell put me in the cabinet. She said 'estate sale,' and later Marisol told me what that means."

"What *is* an estate sale?" asked Annabelle, an unsettling feeling washing over her.

"An estate sale," said Angelica, "is when all the property belonging to a person or family is sold off. I guess the person whose house I was in had died, and everything in the house was put up for sale."

"Including you," said Annabelle.

"Gosh," said Bobby, and Annabelle knew exactly what he was thinking, because it was exactly what *she* was thinking. Annabelle, the great worrier, had somehow never entertained the idea that someday she might not live in the Palmers' house. How could she not have thought of that? She had just assumed that each girl who owned her would one day have a daughter of her own who would want to play with the Dolls and their house. But now Annabelle saw how easily her lovely life could fall apart. Maybe one day, when Kate was older, she would decide to pack up her toys, lock the dollhouse, and put everything in the attic. And then the Doll family would be stuck in the attic until who knew when. Anything could happen. The Palmers might sell their house and forget what was in the attic. And some other family might come across the ancient dollhouse and decide to get rid of it. Why, Annabelle could end up at the dump!

"Annabelle?" said Angelica. "Are you all right? You have the funniest expression on your face."

"I'm okay," replied Annabelle, who was not okay at all.

"Anyway," Angelica continued, "I've been in this display case ever since I got here. I don't think anyone will buy me until I get my mouth fixed. Plus, look at my price tag. I cost a fortune. No one is going to pay so much money for me." She glanced at Annabelle and Bobby and Tilly May and added, "I'll bet you get your price tags today."

"But we're not for sale!" cried Annabelle. "We're here by mistake."

Angelica nodded. "I've heard that before."

"No. Really. We are. We ran away from our home and now we're trying to get back."

"You ran away?"

"Yes," said Annabelle, who had to tell the story again, this time aided by Bobby and occasionally even Tilly. She had just reached the part about the ride in Ms. Lewis's pocket when she saw Angelica stiffen.

"Here comes Marcie," said Angelica. "She's new. She's only been here a week. She likes working at McGinitie's, but she's not very tidy, so she drives Nell crazy." Angelica sighed. "Do you know? Every morning when the store opens I think to myself: Maybe today is the day someone will buy me and I'll finally have another home."

All around Annabelle the last little flutterings of sound died away, and teeny movements came to a halt. The toy department, which had been almost still, was now entirely still; soundless except for Marcie, who banged her pocketbook onto the counter and called out, "Hello, dollies!"

Annabelle's first full day in the toy department may have been long, but it certainly wasn't boring. She felt alarmed every time a customer stepped up to the display case and stared in at the dolls. The first time this happened, and Annabelle suddenly found herself eyeball to eyeball with a stranger, she nearly jumped, but managed to control herself. She wished mightily that she could reach for Bobby's hand, but had instead to remain hanging stiffly from her stand.

All day long customers came and went. Marcie decided to rearrange the dolls in the display case and left it looking messier than before. The computer chirped and binged. Periodically, Viramax would shout, "Batter up! Batter up!" Dolls were handed across the counter, placed in bags, and carried from the store, on their way to new homes. Children laughed. Children threw tantrums. Parents laughed. Parents scolded. People peered in at Annabelle and spoke about her as if she couldn't hear them.

"A shame about her hair," said one, making a face.

"She's pretty," said another. "But, well, she's so *old*."

And a little girl stared and stared at her and finally said to her father, "Does she talk? Does she cry? What does she *do*?"

In the afternoon, Marcie went home and Nell came on duty, and soon afterward, Ms. Lewis strode into the toy department. She was holding three small white tags on strings, and she said, "Nell, I've done some research and I've arrived at prices for the new dolls."

"Wonderful," said Nell.

Moments later the cabinet door was opened, and in reached Ms. Lewis's veiny hand. "Good heavens," she said. "Look at this display. It's a disgrace." She pursed her lips.

"Isn't Marcie supposed to keep this area neat?"

"Yes, but she's still getting the hang of things," said Nell quickly. "I'll talk to her about it."

"Please see that you do." With trembling fingers, Ms. Lewis fastened a price tag to Tilly's stand, then to Bobby's, and finally to Annabelle's.

The Dolls were officially for sale.

That evening, after the cleaning crew had left and Marisol had again taken Annabelle and Bobby and Tilly out of the case, Annabelle ran toward the Funcraft Dream House display, and reached it just as Tiffany scooted out the front door.

"Annabelle!" she cried. "I was kid-napped!"

"I know! I saw. Why did she take you?"

"She said I'm her missing daughter. I tried to tell her who I really am, but she wouldn't believe me. She made me go to my room and lie on the bed. She's very bossy. And strange. She has that mark down her back, and some kid drew giant lashes around her eyes with a felt-tip pen."

"Where is she now?"

"I don't know. I didn't see her when I left the house. I ran out of there as soon as I could. She's a horrible mother. Nothing like my mom. She has all these rules and she would never slide down a banister or do anything fun." Tiffany paused and wrinkled her nose. "It was so weird being in that house that looks just like my house with those people who look just like Bailey and Baby Britney and Mom and Dad, but who are really just creepy rule-followers. Plus, the house was all tidy. I like Nora's messy house." Tiffany glanced over her shoulder at the display Dream House, and Annabelle, feeling as if someone was dripping ice water down her spine, followed her gaze.

"Forget about it," said Annabelle. But then she added, "I wonder why that Mom doll thought you were her Tiffany. Where was her actual Tiffany?"

"I have no idea. Maybe all these Funcraft dolls can't tell each other apart. Come on. Let's get out of here before that mom catches up with me."

Annabelle forgot about this conversation for the next few hours. The dolls spent a second night with Dakota Jane and Elsipad and their other new friends. Bobby and Bailey played baseball again, Viramax continuing to shout, "Batter up! Batter up!" Tilly visited with some of the baby doll Shut-ins. But Annabelle couldn't stop thinking about her home in Kate's room and about the family she'd left behind. She pictured Mama's face, which she was sure was creased with worry, and Baby Betsy, alone and missing her brother and sister. She imagined conversations among the grown-ups, her father pacing the parlor, Nanny fussing. How, wondered Annabelle, how on *earth*, were she and Tiffany and the others going to find their way home?

Before Annabelle knew it, the sun was rising and the cleaning up had begun. Marisol plucked her and Tilly and Bobby from their friends, settled them on their stands next to Angelica and the other old dolls, and closed the door of the case.

Annabelle hung in her spot, her eyes glued to the play area, and waited for Tiffany to be marched away by the creepy Mom Funcraft again. She could tell that her friend was waiting too. Tiffany and Bailey, after helping to finish the cleanup, hopped into a Funcraft school bus and looked out the windows. Annabelle watched Tiffany gaze around and around the play area, expecting the mom to march across the floor at any moment and yank her away. But the toy department settled into stillness, Marcie arrived, and Angelica murmured, "Maybe today is the day."

Another morning at McGinitie's had begun.

When it was over, when the long hours had at last passed, and Marisol (who had nearly been sold that afternoon) had let

Annabelle and the other prisoners in the glass case escape for the evening, Annabelle, with Tilly in tow, made a beeline for Tiffany, who had spent a rigorous day being tossed around the play area.

"Where's the mom?" Annabelle asked, as she and Tiffany clasped hands.

Tiffany looked bewildered. "I don't know. And I think it's a little strange that she didn't show up. She was so strict with me when she dragged me into the house that morning. I'm trying to remember the last time I saw her. I think it was sometime yesterday when a boy started to rearrange the display house."

"Hey, Tiffany! Hey, Annabelle! Hey, Tilly!"

Annabelle looked over her shoulder and saw the red pickup truck roll to a stop behind her. DJ and Elsipad climbed out of the front. "I guess you heard the news," said DJ.

Marisol joined them. "Yeah, you guys look worried."

"You know about the weird mom doll?" said Tiffany.

Elsipad and DJ glanced at each other, then at Marisol.

"What?" said Annabelle warily, watching them. "What is it?"

"Probably nothing," said DJ, "but, well, Mom Funcraft isn't the first doll to disappear around here lately."

"What do you mean?" asked Annabelle. "And how do you know she disappeared? Maybe she was sold."

"Not a doll all by herself from a display house," said Marisol.

"And not the way she looks," added DJ.

"Maybe that boy took her," said Annabelle. "The one who played with the display. Just stuck her in his pocket and walked out of the store."

"I don't think so," said Tiffany. "He had turned me so I was facing the store, and I was watching him when Nell asked him not to touch the display. I'm positive he didn't take anything before he left." Tiffany added ruefully, "Later some other kid put me back on the bed and I couldn't see anything except the ceiling for the rest of the day. Anyway, the mom probably disappeared last night."

Annabelle shivered. She turned to DJ. "What did you mean when you said Mom Funcraft isn't the first doll to disappear?"

"Just that. In the last week, two other dolls who were here during the day were gone by nighttime."

Annabelle heard a small cry escape from her lips. She gripped Tilly May's hand hard.

CHAPTER ELEVEN

The All-Girl Posse

"ANNABELLE, CALM down," said Elsipad. "Remember: don't worry, be happy."

"How can you not worry about this?" replied Annabelle. "It's worrisome."

"If you want to worry about something, worry about how you guys are going to get home," said Dakota Jane. She shook her ponytail.

"I'm worried about that too!" cried Annabelle. "And now I'm worried that one of us will disappear before we can figure out how to find our way back home."

"Excuse me. I couldn't help overhearing you."

Annabelle turned to see Angelica approaching.

"Really, I didn't mean to eavesdrop," said Angelica, "but Annabelle, I think you should try to accept the fact that you're here for good. I've been here longer than any other doll in the store, and as far as I know, no one has ever escaped from McGinitie's."

Annabelle had a sudden inspiration. "Maybe the missing dolls escaped! Maybe that's what happened to them!"

Angelica, Dakota Jane, Elsipad, and Marisol, standing in a ragged line before Annabelle and Tiffany, shook their heads.

"I don't think so," said Marisol.

"No way," said DJ.

"Impossible," said Angelica.

"Nope," said Elsipad, and added, "Annabelle, remember, the dolls here *want* to be sold. They want to go to their Forever Homes. You guys are the only ones who want to escape. Besides . . ." Elsipad waved her hand around the store, and Annabelle knew it was her way of saying, "How could a doll get out of McGinitie's?"

"There must be some way," said Tiffany.

"It couldn't happen during the day," said Elsipad. "How would you go down the escalator?"

"Without being seen," added Marisol.

"It couldn't happen during the night," said DJ. "There's a watchman down-stairs."

"Stationed right beside the entrance," added Angelica.

"Really," said Elsipad, "the only way out of here is in a paper bag."

"What?" said Tiffany.

"Someone has to buy you," Angelica explained.

Annabelle cringed. That was not going to happen to her. Or to her sister or brother or Tiffany or Bailey. They were not going to leave McGinitie's after all this time only to wind up in the wrong house. "That does it," said Annabelle, and she stamped her foot. "We have to get out of here."

"But how are you going to do that?" asked DJ, who, Annabelle thought, looked intrigued by the thought of escape.

Annabelle wanted desperately to impress her, but she felt her shoulders slump. "I don't know." She glanced at Tiffany.

"The main problem," said her best friend, "is not that we don't know how to escape, it's that we don't know how to get back to the Palmers' house."

At the thought of the Palmers' house, Annabelle nearly let loose a sob. It was at this awful moment, feeling helpless and trapped, that Annabelle became aware of a low hum. "What's that?" she asked.

"What's what?" asked Marisol.

"That sound."

Marisol turned in a slow circle, and her eyes settled on a shelf of Dr. Sue dolls, each wired to the back of her cardboard box, along with her doctor's kit and plastic animals. "The Shut-ins," said Marisol. "I think they heard about the disappearance. They're spreading the word among themselves."

Annabelle listened hard and realized that the hum was a chorus of muted voices. "Gone," she heard one doll say. "Gone into the night."

"Into the light?" said another.

"What? In a fright?" said a third.

"Can't hear you," said a fourth. "After a fight?"

"Pardon?" said a fifth. "A fight? Who had a fight?"

DJ leaned over and whispered to Annabelle, "They can't hear very well, not through all that cardboard and cellophane."

"They're apt to spread rumors," added Angelica.

Annabelle looked from the nervous Shut-ins to her friends and then up and down the aisle. She realized that unlike the previous nights, when the atmosphere in the toy department had been cheerful, almost celebratory, the dolls now seemed subdued.

"Where's the baseball game?" Tiffany asked.

"No game tonight," replied Dakota Jane.

"No one felt like playing," said Elsipad.

"Besides, a bunch of the boys have formed a posse," said Marisol.

"A posse? What for?" asked Annabelle.

And Tilly May looked up from her seat on a miniature rocking horse to say, "What's a posse?"

"It's a group of men the sheriff can call on to maintain law and order," replied Dakota Jane, twirling a lariat.

Tiffany made a face. "A group of *men*? What men?"

"And what sheriff?" asked Annabelle.

"Well, there's no sheriff here, of course," said DJ. "Although now that I think of it, someone should make a sheriff doll."

"A *woman* sheriff doll," said Tiffany.

"But who's in this posse?" asked Annabelle.

"All the Bailey dolls and any other boys who want to join," replied DJ.

"They're calling themselves the Bailey Boys," said Elsipad.

"Hmm," said Tiffany. "I wonder just which Bailey had this all-boy idea."

"What are the boys going to do?" asked Angelica.

"Look for Mom Funcraft," said Marisol. "And the other missing dolls."

"And make sure no one else goes missing," said Elsipad.

"They're guarding and patrolling," said DJ.

"How come only the boys get to do this?" asked Tiffany. "What's wrong with girls?"

Elsipad shrugged. "Nothing. The boys had the idea first."

"Well, doesn't anybody think this is

wrong? Girls can guard and patrol just as well as boys," said Tiffany.

"Better," spoke up Tilly, and everyone turned to look at her, but she was busy combing the horse's mane.

"Yeah. That's right!" said Dakota Jane.

"Tell everyone about SELMP," Annabelle said importantly to Tiffany, and Tiffany did so.

"Wow," said Elsipad, Dakota Jane, and Marisol.

Angelica looked fascinated. "I never heard of such a thing," she said. "Not in all my born days."

"I propose," said Tiffany, climbing on top of a building block and raising her fist in the air, "that we form an all-girl posse, and that Annabelle and I make the rest of you"—she pointed at Angelica,

Marisol, Elsipad, and Dakota Jane—"temporary SELMP deputies. Our mission will be to search and guard, protect and patrol. Are you in or are you out?"

"We're in!" cried Annabelle, Marisol, Elsipad, Dakota Jane, and Angelica; Angelica adding, "I never dreamed I'd be deputized."

"I'm in too!" said Tilly May.

Annabelle smiled at her. "You can be a junior deputy."

"Okay, let's go round up some more girls," said Tiffany.

"Wait. Before we start," said Elsipad, "we should have a briefing."

"What?" said Tiffany.

"The dolls who have been here the longest should give you new dolls the lay of the land."

Tiffany looked highly impatient, but she stepped off the block. "All right. I guess that makes sense," she said. "Let's start with the night watchman. You said he's stationed by the entrance. Does he stay there all the time?"

"As far as we know," answered Dakota Jane. She turned to Angelica. "Has he ever come upstairs?"

Angelica shook her head. "Not since I've been here."

"Then that tells us two things," said Tiffany. "We don't have to worry about running into the watchman unless we go downstairs, and the watchman isn't the kidnapper. Okay. What else do we need to know?"

"What about Charlie and the cleaning crew?" asked Annabelle. "Where do they go after they've been in the toy department?"

Everyone looked at Angelica.

"I'm not certain about that," she said. "I know they don't come back here. But I guess they could be anywhere else in the store."

"Well, the good thing about the cleaning crew is that they're noisy," said Tiffany. "We should be able to hear them before we see them. We'll just have to keep our ears open while we're out searching and guarding."

"And protecting and patrolling," added Elsipad.

"Are there any other humans in the store at nighttime?" asked Tiffany.

"I don't think so," said Marisol. "But you do have to be on the lookout for something else."

"What's that?" said Annabelle, an unpleasant feeling coming over her.

Marisol lowered her voice and whispered, "Rats."

"Rats!" shrieked Annabelle, and even Tiffany looked nervous.

The other dolls nodded.

"But we haven't seen any rats," said Tiffany.

"Don't worry. They don't bother us when we're all out at nighttime," said Dakota Jane. "There are too many of us."

"But they're around the store, believe me," added Elsipad. "In dark corners and quiet places."

"Could a rat make off with a doll?" asked Tiffany. "Maybe the kidnapper is a rat."

"It's possible," replied Marisol. "Of course, a rat couldn't make off with *me*. I'm much too big. But you smaller dolls . . ."

Tiffany was quiet for a moment. Then she said, "So, what are the Bailey Boys doing? And where are they?" She looked around the strangely quiet toy department.

"Half of them," replied Elsipad, "were going to go to the top of the escalator to try to see the first floor from up there. They're hoping to spy on the watchman. They want to see if he does anything unusual. The rest of them are supposed to be searching this floor for the missing dolls."

"Then what I think we, as members of SELMP, should do," said Tiffany, "is split up, like the boys did. Half of us can search and explore this floor, too—there'll be plenty for everyone to do. But the other half of us will stay here and guard the toy department. We should probably watch the babies extra closely, since they don't know how to protect themselves."

"Good idea," said DJ.

And so the night passed quickly—and spookily. The members of SELMP rounded up a large group of girl volunteers. Annabelle, Angelica, and Tilly, along with other dolls who were old or fragile, remained behind (with Marisol for protection) to guard the toy department, while Tiffany, Elsipad, Dakota Jane, and a large group of Tiffany Funcrafts and other plastic dolls set off to search the second floor of McGinitie's. Annabelle spent much of the night pacing the aisle of the toy department, hand in hand with Tilly May. She jumped at every sound she heard, every movement she caught out of the corner of her eye. But the hours passed, and Annabelle was able to call, "Two o'clock and all's we-ell!" "Three o'clock and all's we-ell!" until finally she saw the gray light of dawn through the store window.

The rest of the all-girl posse spent the night roaming Housewares, Menswear, Lingerie, and Shoes, on the lookout for rodents and other kidnappers. Dakota Jane drove the truck, with Tiffany and Elsipad in the back, and covered ground quickly. The

other dolls, mostly Tiffanys, searched on foot.
One Tiffany rounded a corner and found
herself facing a shoe. She looked up. A sock
was in the shoe and an ankle was in the sock.
She prepared herself for Doll State, and then
she realized she had encountered a man-
nequin.

Every hour, just after Annabelle called
out her "All's we-ell," DJ drove the truck back
to the toy department to report to Annabelle,
Angelica, and Marisol. On this spooky night,
the dolls, boys and girls alike, saw spiders,
moths, brown mice, and plenty of shadows

obscuring who knew what. They also found (in Housewares) a dollhouse made entirely of gingerbread, which was fun to explore. But neither the Bailey Boys nor the all-girl posse saw rats or anything suspicious. And in the morning, when they gathered in the toy department, they were fairly certain that no more dolls had gone missing.

Annabelle was relieved to return to the glass cabinet.

CHAPTER TWELVE

Where Have All the Dollies Gone?

WHEN THE CLEANING crew left the toy department the next night, the dolls waited only minutes before gathering in the aisle and forming their posses again.

"Look how many of us are here!" exclaimed Tiffany, but her voice was hushed since, by unspoken agreement, the dolls were keeping as quiet as possible.

"Even more than last night," said Annabelle.

"Every single one of us is here," agreed Elsipad, "except for the babies and the Shut-ins. Even the buckets of Tiffanys and Baileys have completely emptied, and you know the ones at the bottom don't always bother to climb out. But tonight they did."

"My goodness," said Tiffany. "This is great. All right, let's divide ourselves into groups and continue searching and patrolling."

And that's what the dolls did. Annabelle, keeping watch in the toy department once more, called out her "all's well"s on the hour. As dawn approached, the posses began to return.

"Nobody saw a thing," reported Tiffany. "Nothing suspicious, anyway."

Annabelle watched the Tiffanys and Baileys line up at the buckets and hurl themselves inside. "I have a funny feeling," she said.

"About what?" asked Marisol, who was waiting to lift Annabelle back into the case.

Annabelle shrugged. "Just a funny feeling."

"Funny good or funny bad?" Tiffany wanted to know.

"Funny bad. Are you sure nobody saw anything?"

"Nobody said they did," Tiffany replied.

And Marisol added, "Two mice, some spiders, and a green insect. Really, Annabelle, nobody saw anything suspicious."

"All right." Annabelle allowed Marisol to place her and Bobby and Tilly May in their spots in the case (different spots than before, since Marcie had once again tried to clean up the case).

Then Angelica was lifted onto a shelf, and she whispered, "Maybe today is the day."

And it nearly was.

Late in the afternoon, during a rush, when so many people crowded the aisle that Annabelle couldn't see the play area beyond, she suddenly found herself looking into the face of a young woman who said excitedly, "Oh, Caroline! What about that one?"

The woman pointed to Angelica, and a small voice from below (Annabelle couldn't lower her eyes to peek at Caroline) replied, "Yes, Mommy! She's perfect! She's just what I wanted. Can we take her out and look at her?"

The woman inspected the case. "I guess so," she replied. "There's no sign that says we can't open it. Let me see if it's locked." She

tugged at the handle and the front of the case
opened.

"Goody!" exclaimed Caroline.

A pair of hands reached for Angelica and
gently removed her from her stand, then shut
the front of the case. The woman leaned
down to hand Angelica to Caroline.

"Can I really have her, Mommy?"
Annabelle heard Caroline say, but by then
she could no longer see Caroline or her
mother or Angelica. Not without moving
her head. Annabelle wished she could cross her
fingers for luck, or turn and wave good-bye
to her friend, but she contented herself with
a silent chant: *Please let Angelica have a new home,
please let Angelica have a new home.*

She had just decided that today truly was
Angelica's lucky day when she noticed
Caroline's mother
again, this time
farther down
the aisle so that
now Annabelle
could see Caroline
too (she assumed
the little girl was
Caroline)—and

neither Caroline nor her mother was carrying a McGinitie's shopping bag.

Caroline was trying very hard not to cry.

"I'm sorry," her mother said. "I'm very
sorry, honey. But I couldn't read the price tag
without my glasses. I didn't realize the dolly
was so expensive. We simply can't afford
to spend that much money on a
doll."

Annabelle heaved an imaginary sigh. Poor Angelica. She was to be returned to the glass case once again. Annabelle waited for Nell to bring her back, and she rehearsed what she would say to Angelica that evening after the cleaning crew had left. Something cheerful and uplifting like, "There's bound to be a little girl or boy who will want you. You'll find a home one day; I know you will."

Annabelle was working on an analogy about how lots of good things take time—the writing of a book, the growth of a tree, the building of a home, and so forth—when she looked at the clock and realized that Angelica had been out of the case for more than half an hour. Why hadn't Nell brought her back? Maybe someone else had come along and bought her, reflected Annabelle. It seemed unlikely, but you never knew.

Annabelle took a chance and cut her eyes, ever so slightly, to the left, trying to glimpse the checkout counter. She caught sight of the tip of Angelica's shoe. So she hadn't been sold. Well, it was a busy day, Annabelle thought. The aisle was still crammed with shoppers. Nell must not have had time to put Angelica away.

Confident that she would see her friend soon, Annabelle returned to the speech she was rehearsing, determined to be ready to comfort Angelica that evening.

When Marisol opened the case that night, the first thing she said to Annabelle was, "Where's Angelica?"

"Over on the counter, I think," Annabelle replied, straining to see.

Marisol turned her head in that direction. "No, she isn't."

"Are you sure?"

"Positive." Marisol glanced around the toy department. "I don't see her anywhere."

"Well, that's strange," said Annabelle, and she told Marisol what had happened that afternoon. "The mother decided Angelica was too expensive, so they left without her. I saw them. The girl was almost crying. And she definitely didn't have a shopping bag with her."

"Why did you think Angelica was on the counter?" asked Bobby, who'd been listening. "You can't see the counter from the display case."

Annabelle hesitated. "I just moved my eyes the teeniest, teeniest little bit," she admitted.

"Annabelle!" exclaimed Marisol and Bobby.

And Marisol added, "In front of all the shoppers?"

"No one was looking at me. Anyway, it was when the store was so busy. All the humans were hurrying along, bumping into each other, pulling things off the shelves. I really wanted to see what had happened to Angelica. And I saw the tip of her shoe. At least, I thought it was Angelica's shoe."

"But where is she now?" asked Bobby.

"Maybe someone shoplifted her!" cried Annabelle.

Marisol had deposited Annabelle, Bobby, and Tilly May on the floor and was now lifting dolls down from other shelves and displays.

"Shoplifted who?" asked Tiffany, who was running across the aisle, followed by Elsipad and Dakota Jane.

"Angelica," replied Annabelle, and she had to tell the story a second time.

"She wasn't shoplifted," said DJ. "She lay on the counter for the rest of the afternoon."

"Well, she isn't there now," said Annabelle. "Oh," she moaned. "I said this morning I had a funny feeling, and this is why. Angelica is the next missing doll."

"We don't know that," said Elsipad.

"Don't we?" countered Annabelle. "Where is she?" When no one could answer her question, she repeated, "She *is* the next missing doll."

The toy department was a quiet place that night. Only a few posses went patrolling. The rest of the dolls stayed behind, talking quietly. There was no baseball game, no picnic. Many of the Tiffanys and Baileys elected to remain in the buckets.

"They're probably safer that way," remarked Annabelle.

It was just after midnight when Elsipad, riding in DJ's truck with Annabelle, Tiffany, and Tilly, said, "Have you guys seen the twins lately?"

"No," replied the others.

After a pause, Elsipad asked, "Well, when was the last time anyone saw them?"

"I'm not sure," said Tiffany.

"Maybe last night?" suggested DJ. She leaned her head out the truck window to look at the dolls riding in the back, and turned around again just in time to avoid running into a Funcraft Dream House.

"Did they go out with the posses?" asked Annabelle.

The others shrugged.

"I didn't pay much attention to the Bailey Boys," admitted DJ.

A hush fell. DJ let the truck wind down, and everybody hopped out. "Go ask around," said DJ, sounding serious.

Annabelle and her friends hurried from one group of dolls to another, asking them if they knew where Vixamax and Viramax were, or when they remembered seeing them.

No one had seen the twins since the last baseball game.

"That was three nights ago," whispered Annabelle. She looked up and down the aisle. Then she began to run from one row of shelves to another.

"What is it? What's the matter?" asked Tiffany.

"Where are Bobby and Bailey?"

"I saw them just a minute ago."

"Bobby! Bailey!" Annabelle called, heart pounding. "*Bobby!*"

"Bobby! Bobby!" called Tilly May.

"What?" replied two muffled voices. A moment later, Bobby and Bailey poked their heads out of a plastic airplane.

"We thought you had disappeared!" exclaimed Annabelle.

"No, *you* thought they had disappeared," said Tiffany.

"Can you blame me?" Annabelle turned to her brother and Bailey. "Now the twins are missing too," she said.

"Uh-oh." Bobby and Bailey plopped onto the floor.

Annabelle looked around at the frightened faces of her brother and sister, of Tiffany and Bailey and DJ and Elsipad. Then

she looked at the marks on the foreheads of
Tiffany and Bailey.

And then she put her hand to her
mouth and gasped.

"Annabelle?" said Elsipad.

Annabelle drew in a deep breath. "I just
realized something," she said. "The dolls who
disappeared—at least, the ones who have disappeared since we've been here—are . . .
well, they have something in common."

Tiffany frowned. "They do? What?"

Annabelle paused. "I don't want to be rude," she said, "but . . . they aren't perfect."

"None of us is perfect," said Elsipad primly.

"That's not what I mean." It was Annabelle's turn to frown. "Think about it. The Mom Funcraft doll had that mark on her back, and the drawn-on eyelashes. Angelica's smile had worn off. And Viramax had that . . . whatever you call it. That glitch in his system."

"What about Vixamax?" asked Elsipad.

Annabelle frowned. "I don't know. It's true: nothing's wrong with him. But it's interesting that he's Viramax's twin, isn't it? And something is wrong with Viramax, and they're both missing."

For a few moments everyone was quiet. Then Bailey said, "We don't know that the twins weren't sold."

"But we know that Mom and Angelica weren't sold," said Annabelle. "And you have to admit it's strange that there's something wrong with almost all the missing dolls."

"Yes," said Bailey uncomfortably.

"It must be rats," said Bobby. "Rats are taking the dolls."

"Rats that choose imperfect dolls?" replied Annabelle.

Everyone was silent again, this time for so long that finally Tilly said, "I fought only free-year-old girl dolls were allowed to play the quiet game."

Annabelle smiled and drew her sister close.

"What do you think is happening to these imperfect dolls?" asked Dakota Jane.

Annabelle shook her head. "I don't know. Maybe they're being discarded."

"Discarded!" yelped Elsipad.

"Maybe," said Annabelle again. And then she added, "Tiffany, you have to rub those initials off of your forehead and Bailey's. If my theory is right, they make you targets."

Tiffany opened her mouth. She closed it again. Then she opened it and said quietly, "Annabelle, what about your hair?"

CHAPTER THIRTEEN

A Close Call

Annabelle's hand flew to her hair, her green hair. "Oh . . . oh, my," she whispered. "I never thought . . ." Then she drew herself up straight and pictured her Auntie Sarah. If Auntie Sarah were there, she would clap her hands together and say briskly, "Well, it can't be helped. We can't paint your hair. Let's focus on the things we *can* change."

Annabelle faced her friends. "There's nothing to be done about my hair," she told them. "But we can take care of Tiffany and Bailey, and we'd better do it right away."

Tiffany looked panicked. "What are we going wash the letters off with? Anything we use is going to get dirty, and we can't make something dirty that wasn't dirty before."

"You would have had the same problem at the Palmers'," Annabelle pointed out. She was very frightened, and feeling frightened made her feel cross as well.

"Come on, you guys, don't fight," said DJ. "Annabelle, being in a big store is different from living in someone's house. Look. There's a tissue on the floor that the cleaning people missed. You can use that. No one will know the difference."

Tiffany dove for the Kleenex and, with the help of Annabelle and the others, managed to scrub most of the crayon from Bailey's forehead and her own.

"Good. You'd never notice the marks now," said Elsipad. "I can only see them because I know where they were." She turned to Annabelle. "I wish you could wear a hat."

"So do I."

But they all knew that Annabelle could no more turn up in the display case the next day wearing a hat than she could with a repainted head.

Tilly May, who didn't understand what was happening, bounced up and down and began to sing, "Ain't a-gonna need this house no longer, ain't a-gonna need this house no more." She looked around at the others. "Rosemary Clooney Favorites," she announced.

Annabelle barely heard her. "You know what?" she said. "I just figured out that this is the sixth night we've been away from home."

Tiffany nodded. Then she said, her eyes fixed on the floor, "We've been saying this all along, but now it's more important than ever: We *have* to escape from McGinitie's."

"I think," said Annabelle, "that we can find a way to escape. But how are we going to get back to the Palmers' house? We don't know where it is."

This was followed by a long, long silence, which Annabelle took as a bad sign.

At last Elsipad said, without much confidence, "Where there's a will, there's a way."

Just before Marisol returned Annabelle and her brother and sister to the case that morning,

Tiffany said, "Our job today is to think—really *think*—about how to return to the Palmers' house. Elsipad is right: there must be a way, and we have to make sure we have the will to find it."

"Visualize escaping," called Elsipad over her shoulder as she returned to her display.

And that is what Annabelle was doing that afternoon (Saturday, Annabelle realized with a shock, which meant the Palmers would return from their vacation in exactly one week) when she once again found herself looking into the face of a shopper. It was a woman, and she had followed a girl who had stepped off the escalator and walked directly to the glass case.

"There," said the girl, and she pointed to Annabelle.

This girl was taller and older than the girl named Caroline. She was, thought Annabelle, about Kate Palmer's age.

The girl glanced at the woman, then looked at Annabelle again. "I saw that doll here the other day," she said. "I want her for my collection."

The woman looked dubiously at

Annabelle. "Are you *sure*, Maggie?" she said. "She has green hair."

"Mo-om! Yes! I want her."

Annabelle was positive that if Kate had used that tone of voice around her parents or Grandma Katherine, she would have been whisked out of McGinitie's and taken straight home.

But Maggie's mother said, "All right," and opened the glass case and withdrew Annabelle. Maggie grabbed her, and just like

that, Annabelle was closed into a sweaty hand, and the hand began to swing back and forth as Maggie marched through the toy department, away from Bobby, away from Tilly. Annabelle forcibly stopped herself from picturing Tilly watching helplessly as her big sister was snatched from under her very nose.

"And there's the bead set I want," Annabelle heard Maggie say a moment later.

"Which one? The one on top of the stack?" asked her mother.

"No! I told you—the one with the purple beads. *That* one."

Annabelle, staring (upside down) through the crack between Maggie's fourth finger and her pinky, saw Maggie point to a box on a shelf. Another hand (belonging to Maggie's mother, Annabelle assumed) slid the box out from the middle of the pile.

"Okay," said the mother with a sigh. "Let's find a checkout counter."

"There's one," said Maggie. "But no one's at the register."

"Well, we'll just have to wait."

"I *hate* waiting," Maggie whined. "Oh, look! American iDolls! I want an—"

"Maggie," her mother snapped. "No. You can't have *every*thing. We came here to get the doll and the bead set."

"But I want an iDoll too!"

"No."

Maggie was now clutching Annabelle around the throat, which was better than being squeezed into her hand, because at least Annabelle could see properly. And what she saw was Maggie stamping her foot over and over, then jumping up and down, and then screeching, "But I *want* everything!"

"We all do, dear," said her mother. After a moment she added, "And if you don't stop screaming, we are going to walk out of here with nothing." She placed the bead set on the counter.

"Fine!" cried Maggie. "Get me nothing. See if I care. You don't love me!"

Annabelle wasn't quite certain about what happened in the next few moments. There was a tremendous crash (it felt tremendous to Annabelle, at any rate) as her body was slammed onto the counter. The slam was accompanied by an ominous crack. Annabelle was vaguely aware of Maggie and her mother as they huffed out of the toy department, but she paid little attention to them.

A web of gray lines had appeared on her right hand, and Annabelle knew it was broken. She lay on her side against the box of beads. One leg was crossed over the other, and her arm, the one with the broken hand, stuck out straight ahead, as if she were pointing at Maggie.

A figure loomed above Annabelle, and she made out the indignant face of Nell calling, "Ma'am! Ma'am! Excuse me!" But already Annabelle could see only the top of Maggie's head as she disappeared down the escalator, two outraged steps behind her mother.

Nell turned her attention to Annabelle. "Well, of all the nerve," she said. "Taking one of the antique dolls out of the case and just leav—" Nell leaned over for a closer look. "Why, they broke it!" she exclaimed. (Annabelle presumed that she was the "it.") Nell ran to the top of the escalator, paused, then returned to Annabelle, who guessed that Maggie and her mother were already out of sight. "I swan," said Nell under her breath. "Some people . . ." Nell picked Annabelle up gently and turned her over and over, examining her carefully. Then she nodded, seeming, Annabelle thought, to come to some sort of decision. "All right," said Nell at last, and with Annabelle resting in the palm of her hand, she walked swiftly through the second floor of McGinitie's.

Annabelle watched Housewares fly by, and then Lingerie—and a horrifying thought entered her head: Suppose she too was to be discarded? She was imperfect, after all. Her hair was one thing, but now her hand was cracked. She was no longer fit to be displayed in a great glass case. She was damaged merchandise. Perhaps this was what had happened to Angelica, to Viramax and Vixamax, to the Mom doll. Nell or one of the other clerks had simply picked them up and, unnoticed by the other dolls, discarded them. On the other hand, why didn't Nell just drop Annabelle into the nearest wastebasket? Why carry her through McGinitie's?

Nell sailed through Lingerie, and suddenly Annabelle knew where they were headed: the Up Escalator. Sure enough, Nell carried Annabelle to the third floor, around through Infants, and then up another flight to the fourth floor. In her week at McGinitie's Annabelle had heard about the fourth floor—which was home to all sorts of miscellaneous departments, such as gift-wrapping and customer service—but she didn't know of any doll who had actually been there. Why, Annabelle wondered, was she being taken there now?

When Nell finally came to a stop, it was before a closed door. Annabelle had a good view of the door, since she was resting on her side on Nell's open palm. Two words were written on the door.

Huh. A hospital. Annabelle remembered when Kate was three and had had her tonsils removed. The surgery had taken place at a hospital, and so had the removal of a licorice jelly bean from Nora's nose when she was two. The hospital, in both instances, was called

Mercy Hospital—for humans. But was it possible, was it really possible, that there was such a place as a hospital for dolls?

Nell rapped twice on the door, which was open, stuck her head inside, and called, "Yoohoo!"

"Nell, is that you?" a voice replied, although Annabelle couldn't see who was speaking. "I'll be right with you."

Nell set Annabelle on a counter and waited, tapping her fingers. Presently, a woman with a kind face and gray hair, wearing the thickest spectacles Annabelle had ever seen, appeared on the other side of the counter. "Hello," she said. "What do we have here?"

"One of our antique dolls," Nell replied. "If you can believe it, a customer broke it and ran off without offering to pay. See? Look at this hand. Cracked. Do you think you can fix it?"

The woman, who was wearing a name tag that said MRS. KATZ, replied, "It can definitely be fixed. I'll give this job to Sandy. She'll be in on Monday. I'll call you to let you know when the job has been done."

"Thank you," said Nell, and she left.

Mrs. Katz placed Annabelle on a shelf

and then she disappeared through a door marked WORKROOM. Annabelle looked to her left and right in alarm. She had been set down not amid other dolls, but amid doll *parts*— heads, limbs, and even eyeballs. Annabelle gulped. She tried to collect her thoughts, which were quite scattered. First she thought, This reminds me a little of the doll maker's shop in London. Then she thought, Oh dear, if the person named Sandy doesn't come in until Monday, I might not be repaired until Tuesday or Wednesday—and the Palmers come home on Saturday.

Then she thought, what if Tilly or

Bobby or Tiffany or Bailey is sold while I'm up here in the hospital? Then she thought, My, I was nearly sold myself. That was a close call. Then she thought, What is Tilly going to do tonight without me to look after her? And *then* she thought, I wonder what Baby Betsy is doing right now. And Mama and Papa. They must be frantic with worry. Auntie Sarah and Uncle Doll and Nanny too. And Tiffany's family, of course. What do they think happened to us? And what might happen to them if the Palmers come home before we do?

This last thought was so frightening that Annabelle had to stop thinking. Instead she looked around at the other dolls waiting (she supposed) to be repaired. And that was when she noticed first Angelica, then Mom Funcraft, and finally Viramax and Vixamax. Annabelle felt relieved—the missing dolls were here, and they were going to be repaired! But her relief turned to confusion. Who had brought them here, and why? Annabelle had been brought here because something had happened to her. But nothing had happened to the others, nothing new, anyway. Angelica's smile, for instance, had been gone for years. And Viramax had been yelling "Batter up!" since before Annabelle had first met the twins. Annabelle guessed that most of the other dolls on the shelves already belonged to children, children who loved them so much that they sent them to the doll hospital when they needed fixing. That made sense. But what about the dolls who had disappeared from the toy department? Annabelle was glad to know that they were safe, but she felt very puzzled.

Mrs. Katz was still out of sight, so Annabelle felt she could freely allow her eyes to roam the hospital. None of the dolls on the shelves were moving or speaking, of course. That would have been dangerous with Mrs. Katz so close at hand. But Annabelle didn't see any harm in taking a good look around. She saw mostly old dolls like herself and Angelica, and several beautiful Madame Alexander dolls, and a few newer plastic dolls like Mom Funcraft. And then . . .

Annabelle caught sight of something so terrifying that she nearly gasped. Quickly she looked away, but she felt her eyes drawn back to the terrifying thing as if it were a magnet.

Sitting on a shelf directly across the room from Annabelle was a Princess Mimi doll that looked alarmingly like Mean Mimi: Mean Mimi, who had followed Annabelle and Tiffany back to the Palmers' after their adventure at the boy's house; Mean Mimi, who had tormented Annabelle and Tiffany and their families, and who had done something so awful—right in front of Nora—that she had gone into Permanent Doll State. Eventually, Kate had taken her to the Lost and Found bin at school, and Mimi hadn't been seen since. But Annabelle had often wondered if Mimi had truly gone into PDS, or if she had been pretending. Was it possible that this Princess Mimi doll, the one now staring blankly at Annabelle, was actually *Mean* Mimi? Annabelle, shaken, studied her. Her crown was dented. Her wand was broken. One of her legs had come off and was lying across her lap. What had happened? Had she been pulled from the Lost and Found by her owner or some other child

and brought here for repair? If this was Mean Mimi, and if she was not, in fact, in PDS, she would surely recognize Annabelle Doll.

Inwardly, Annabelle shuddered. What would happen in a few hours when McGinitie's closed and Mrs. Katz turned off the lights and the dolls in the hospital were locked in together?

CHAPTER FOURTEEN

The Return of Mean Mimi

MRS. KATZ bustled out of the workroom, tidied up the counter in the doll hospital, then paused and took one good long look around the room. Her eyes traveled over every shelf. Satisfied, she nodded. Then she turned off the light and closed the door behind her. The doll hospital was plunged into darkness.

Annabelle drew in a deep breath. She waited. And presently she realized that there was a bit of light in the room after all. Two small windows along the side wall let in moonbeams and the glow from streetlamps. Annabelle, her eyes once again drawn to the

Princess Mimi doll, recalled the terrifying visit she and Tiffany had mistakenly paid to the boy's house. It seemed like a very long time ago, although in fact it had taken place less than a year earlier. Annabelle and Tiffany had gone to school in Kate's backpack one morning, had crawled out of it to do a little exploring, and at the end of the day, had accidentally returned to the wrong backpack. They had ended up riding home with a boy called BJ and had spent the weekend at his house. They soon learned that the dolls there were terrorized by a Princess Mimi doll who had no regard for the rules governing dollkind. With great relief, Annabelle and Tiffany had left BJ's house in his backpack on Monday morning, found Kate's backpack at school, and returned to their own homes that afternoon. But Annabelle had had the fright of her life when, not long after she and Tiffany had been blissfully reunited with their worried families, she had heard a small scratching sound, and out of a hidden compartment in Kate's backpack had crawled Mean Mimi herself. The menace had traveled to Annabelle's home.

Mimi had stayed at the Palmers' house for days, putting Annabelle and her friends and family in danger time and again. Then one day she had leaped from a shelf in

full view of Nora, and had instantly been thrust into what the dolls came to believe was Permanent Doll State. She had lain unmoving on Kate's desk until finally Kate had taken her to school and left her in the Lost and Found bin. And that was the last Annabelle had seen or heard of Mean Mimi—until Annabelle had been placed on the shelf in the doll hospital.

Now Annabelle was once again facing the small doll with the wild red hair, the lavender dress, the crown studded with plastic jewels, and the wand topped with the sparkly star. However, as Annabelle had noticed earlier, one of Mimi's legs had come off, the crown was dented, and the wand was broken nearly in two. She looked, Annabelle thought, exactly as she might look after spending a few months buried in a Lost and Found bin. Maybe, Annabelle reflected, BJ's sister had spotted Mimi in the bin at school, had taken her home, and had begged her parents to have her repaired at the doll hospital. This was fine. As long as Mimi was truly in PDS. But if she wasn't, and if that was Mean Mimi up there . . .

(If you're afraid of Mean Mimi, STOP READING RIGHT HERE and skip to the end of this chapter! If you're not afraid, then keep reading . . . at your own risk.)

Annabelle stared at Princess Mimi and saw that the doll was glaring back at her. She nearly let out a yelp. Whoever that doll was, she certainly was *not* in PDS.

Annabelle glanced around at the other dolls on the shelves. They weren't moving yet, and she wondered how long dolls had to hold their positions after lights out in the hospital. Maybe the cleaning crew would be arriving soon, and it was necessary for the dolls to wait until they had left before speaking and stretching their limbs. Oh, how Annabelle longed to leap into Angelica's arms and pour out the story of Mean Mimi, to hear Angelica say to her, "Oh, I'm *sure* that doll isn't *Mean Mimi*, Annabelle." But Annabelle could only sit unmoving on the shelf, Mimi glaring at her from across the room.

And then, before Annabelle's astonished eyes, Mimi suddenly stood up, wobbling on her one leg. Annabelle looked wildly around the doll hospital again, but as before, the other dolls sat stiffly on the shelves.

Does no one else see what's happening? wondered Annabelle. At any moment the door to the hospital could open and in could

walk one of the cleaning crew or Mrs. Katz—
and there would be Mimi, rising from her
shelf.

Annabelle swallowed a shriek and
watched as Mimi bent over, picked up her
other leg, and hoisted it above her head. The
leg held aloft, she hopped to the end of
the shelf, stumping over dolls, stepping on
dresses and stumbling across feet, all the while
keeping her eyes on Annabelle.

At the end of the shelf, Mimi took a great leap and landed on the counter near the cash register. Then she bumped along until she was standing directly across the room from Annabelle. "So," she said. "We meet again, Annabelle Doll."

Annabelle was reminded of the raccoon in the woods, and had the same thought now that she had had as she huddled in the smelly tent: Maybe if I hold very still she'll lose interest in me and go away.

Annabelle averted her eyes just a bit so that she was looking off to Mimi's left, then stiffened herself even further.

"You can't fool me, Annabelle," said Mimi. "I know who you are, and I know what you did to me."

Annabelle was fully aware that she had done not a thing to Mimi. Mimi had done a fine job of getting herself into trouble. She hadn't needed help from anyone else. But Annabelle was not going to be pulled into Mimi's trap. She neither moved nor answered.

Mimi, leaning unsteadily against a stack of *Doll World* magazines, thrust her leg

(Annabelle realized that the foot was missing its ribboned slipper) toward Annabelle, holding it in her outstretched hands. "Do you see this?" called Mimi. "Do you *see* it?" Her voice was taking on the cackling tones of the Wicked Witch of the West from *The Wizard of Oz*, a movie Annabelle had seen in the Palmers' living room when the humans had been out and Tiffany had found both the *TV Guide* and the remote control. Annabelle had been frightened of the witch, but she was more frightened of Mimi.

"*This*," Mimi continued, "is what happens when someone throws you in a Lost and Found can like a piece of garbage. THIS!"

Annabelle stared hard at the leg. Was it moving on its own? Just a little? She thought perhaps it was. She thought perhaps the toes were wiggling.

"So you know what I think?" screeched Mimi. "I think maybe the same thing should happen to you, Annabelle Doll. Little Miss Smarty Pants. Little Miss I'm So Delicate. Little Miss I'm a Hundred Years Old. 'Oh, save me, Tiffany, save me.' Well, Tiffany isn't here to protect you, is she? And that's really a

shame, because you know what I think should happen right now? I think someone should rip *your* leg off. An eye for an eye, a leg for a leg."

Annabelle began to tremble. It was bad enough that her hand was cracked. But Annabelle's legs couldn't just pop out of their sockets the way Mimi's could. If Mimi ripped Annabelle's leg off, she would have to tear it from her fabric body. Annabelle imagined the sound she would hear as the ancient threads were pulled apart and the stuffing leaked out of the ragged hole.

"Hmm," said Mimi. She set the leg upside down on the counter, and leaned on it as if it were a cane. "Hmm. I wonder who, exactly, should have the pleasure of ripping your leg off."

Annabelle kept her eyes on the leg, in particular on the toes. Yes, they were definitely wiggling. A moment later, Mimi stopped talking, glanced down at the foot, and smacked the toes with her left hand. "Hold still," she hissed to them. "I need to concentrate."

The toes went limp.

Mimi looked at Annabelle again. "Now," she said, "I could send one of my minions after you. Oh, yes. I have minions here, just like I did at BJ's. Half the dolls in this room are in my power. Or I could go over there and take care of you myself. . . . What? You think I can't climb onto your shelf?" she asked, even though Annabelle had said nothing. "Well,

I've developed super-doll powers. Yes, I have.
That's what happens when you lie buried in a
Lost and Found bin for months under old
socks and mittens, and lunch boxes that reek
of sour milk and bananas. Do you
know what stared me in the
face for four entire
months, Annabelle
Doll? A sock
m o n k e y
with the
                                                    stupidest smile
                                                  on its little embroi-
                                              dered lips that I've ever
seen. Four months with lifeless button eyes
practically touching my own beautiful ones.

"It wasn't so bad, though, and do you
know why? Because while I was suffering,
something wonderful was happening. My
powers were growing and strengthening, and
now—now I could leap over to your shelf in
one bound and rip off your leg before you
even knew what had happened.

"But I'm not going to do that. No. I
don't think that would be scary enough to pay
you back, Miss Follower of the Rules, Miss Oh

Dear Me No We Mustn't Move Until All the Humans Have Been Asleep For an Hour. No, I'm going to send someone else to do the job. Correction. I'm going to send some*thing* else to do the job. And what am I going to send? *What am I going to send*?" Mimi's voice was rising again. "THIS!" Mimi grabbed her leg and aimed it like a missile at Annabelle.

The leg sailed through the air, the sole of the foot on a direct path with Annabelle's legs, and Annabelle imagined the toes gripping her thigh and pulling and pulling and pulling until . . .

At last Annabelle let out the shriek she'd been holding in for so long. As she did, and before the last high-pitched note had completely faded away, she saw that nothing was flying through the room toward her, nothing at all. And the Princess Mimi doll was not standing on the counter leaning against the magazines. She was sitting on the shelf where Annabelle had first noticed her, her leg lying across her lap. Further-more, her large blue eyes weren't glaring at anything. Annabelle now realized that they were the lifeless, unmoving eyes of a doll who is either in PDS, or who has never taken the oath.

"Annabelle," whispered Angelica. "Hush. We can't talk yet. Not for another hour or so until the cleaning crew has been here."

Annabelle merely nodded her head. She felt foolish. She'd had a dream, a bad dream. Worse than Dorothy's in *The Wizard of Oz*, she decided. But a dream, nevertheless. She slid back on the shelf until she was leaning against the wall, and waited for the cleaning crew to arrive.

CHAPTER FIFTEEN

Extreme Makeover: Doll Edition

Half an hour after the cleaning crew had left, Annabelle felt a familiar shift in the atmosphere of the doll hospital. Around her, dolls began to stir and murmur, and within a few minutes, the hospital had come to life, although not in quite as spectacular a fashion as the toy department came to life, since without Marisol's help, the dolls on the high shelves had great difficulty climbing to the floor. Many of them didn't bother.

"Angelica!" Annabelle cried. "How did you get here? What happened? And what are the twins and the mom doll doing here?"

Angelica attempted a smile. "There's a very simple explanation," she said.

"Yes. You were kidnapped," replied Annabelle. She glanced at the Princess Mimi doll, but Mimi had neither moved nor spoken. She stared straight ahead with dull eyes.

"Not exactly. Someone did take us, but we weren't kidnapped."

"I don't understand," said Annabelle.

"You know Charlie?" asked Angelica.

Annabelle frowned. "Charlie from the cleaning crew?"

"Yes. He brought us here. I mean, he brought the twins and Mom and me and a couple of other dolls from downstairs. The rest of the dolls were brought to the hospital by their owners."

"But *why* did Charlie bring you here?"

"Because he wanted . . ." Angelica paused, thinking. Then she said, "Charlie takes his job very seriously. He's the head of the cleaning crew, you know, and he's new to the job. He's only been working here a few weeks and he wants to make a good impression. Have you noticed that he doesn't just mop and dust and move on? He takes his time and tidies up. He even has a motto, like Elsipad. Only his is 'A place for everything and everything in its place.' But it goes beyond that. Charlie fixes things, too. If a shelf is crooked, he straightens it. If a table leg is wobbly, he tightens it."

"And," said Annabelle, suddenly understanding, "if something is wrong with a doll, he brings it to the hospital."

"Yes," replied Angelica. "He saw the mom doll and brought her here to have those marks removed. And he kept hearing Viramax shout 'Batter up!' which he knew wasn't right. I think he brought Vixamax along just in case he developed the same problem."

"And he brought you here to have your smile repainted."

"Exactly. He saw me lying on the counter the day I was almost sold. Nell had forgotten to put me away, and I think Charlie was going to return me to the case, but then he noticed my mouth and he brought me up here instead. Nobody else ever bothered to do that, but Charlie thinks of those things. You know what, Annabelle? Thanks to Charlie, I'll probably get a new owner right away. I know I'm expensive, but when people see me with a smile, well, I don't think I'll be stuck in that case much longer. Isn't that good news?"

"It's wonderful," said Annabelle, trying to sound enthusiastic.

"You don't seem very happy," said Angelica.

"I'm happy for *you* . . ." Annabelle watched Viramax and Vixamax make their way to the end of a low shelf where Mom Funcraft had been placed. "Truly I am," continued Annabelle. "I was just thinking about what a mess *I'm* in now. Worse than before. Way worse than before."

"Why is it worse? You're going to have your hair repainted. Isn't that a good th— Oh! Oh, I see. You don't want to have your hair fixed because if you find your way home then your owners will notice and—" Angelica stopped speaking and exclaimed, "Annabelle! My goodness! What happened to your hand? Is *that* why you're here? I just assumed it was because of your hair. Oh, I'm so sorry."

"That's okay," said Annabelle, and she told Angelica the story of spoiled Maggie. Then she added, "But now, Angelica, don't you see? I probably won't get out of here until sometime next week, and the Palmers are going to be returning from their vacation on Saturday. And for all I know, by the time I get back to the toy department, Bobby or Tilly or Tiffany or Bailey may have been sold. We might all be split up."

"Hey!" Vixamax called from below. He

had left Viramax with Mom Funcraft, and was now stooped over a piece of paper on the counter. It was on top of a small stack of

papers, and he lifted it up and examined it in the pale moonlight. "This is about you, Annabelle," he said.

"About me? What is it? And how do you know it's about me?"

"It's Mrs. Katz's instructions for the person who's going to fix you next week. Your work order," said Vixamax importantly. "There's a work order for every doll in here so that the repairs will be done properly. And I know this one is yours because where it says 'Item' Mrs. Katz filled in 'Doll with green hair.' Who else could that be?"

Annabelle scowled. "No one."

Vixamax studied the paper. "Wow," he said after a few moments. "Annabelle, you're not just going to have your hand fixed, you're going to get a makeover."

"What?!" exclaimed Annabelle.

"Yeah. There's a long list here. And the first thing on it is 'Repaint hair.'"

"Get a makeover?! Repaint my hair?! But I can't go back to the Palmers' house with a makeover."

Even as Annabelle felt panic rising, Vixamax continued speaking. "Let's see. You're going to get a new dress to replace the . . . what does it say here? To replace the 'faded and yellowing garments.' It will be blue gingham with brown buttons. And your eyes are going to be repainted to give you a 'bolder, perkier look.'"

Annabelle was speechless.

"Do you want me to go on?" asked Vixamax. "There's more."

"No!" cried Angelica. "Don't say another word. This is terrible. Look how upset Annabelle is."

"I'm sorry," said Vixamax, who did indeed sound sorry. "But I thought you'd want to know."

"Yes, you're right," said Angelica quickly. "Annabelle does need to know."

"What are we going to *do*?" wailed Annabelle.

"For starters, calm down," said Vixamax. "Viramax, come here. Mom, you too. We need to talk to Annabelle and Angelica."

The twins and Mom Funcraft made their way across the counter and up the shelves to Annabelle, who was huddled miserably, knees drawn up, head buried in her hands.

"I *have* to get out of here," said Annabelle before they had even sat down. "And not in a few days, but *as soon as possible*. Before anybody touches one green hair on my head. I'm *serious!*" she cried when she glanced up and saw Angelica try to smile again.

"Batter up!" exclaimed Viramax.

Mom Funcraft eyed Annabelle critically. "I really don't see what the problem is," she said after a moment. "Why would you want green hair? Why would you want to stand out? I like looking exactly like all the other Moms." She reached up to pat her own hair.

Annabelle just stared at her. "But I can't go home looking different." She paused. "Did you not take the oath?"

"Annabelle, really, don't panic," said Vixamax. "I have an idea. Tomorrow is Sunday, but the store is open in the afternoon. The hospital is open then too, and someone named Miss Hollis comes in. She's supposed to repair Viramax and take a look at me. And I heard Mrs. Katz ask her to return us to the toy department on her way out. I don't know why, but she did, and that's good for us."

"Okay," said Annabelle.

"So tomorrow night we'll come back and rescue you."

"Really?" said Annabelle. "That would be

wonderful. But how are you going to . . . I mean, there are so many . . . How will you get up the escalator? And how will you get in here? Isn't the door locked?"

"Obstacles," muttered Mom Funcraft. "Messy. I don't like messes."

"I think we can deal with the obstacles," said Angelica.

Annabelle nodded. An image of Auntie Sarah had come into her mind, and Annabelle knew that obstacles wouldn't stop her aunt.

Vixamax grinned at her. "I agree. All right. Let's think."

"We must be tidy. Very tidy," said Mom.

"I know one good thing," spoke up Angelica. "The cleaning crew comes in much earlier on Sunday evening and doesn't stay very long, so you'll have more time for the rescue operation."

"A longer night," agreed Vixamax.

"Operation XL!" Mom Funcraft exclaimed suddenly.

Everyone turned to look at her.

"What?" said Annabelle.

"Hey!" exclaimed Viramax. "That's a

good idea. Operation XL is one of the games that can be downloaded into Vixamax and me. And it's all about a rescue operation."

"Has it been downloaded into you?" asked Annabelle.

"Yes. Let me see what information I can retrieve from it. A moment, please." Vixamax

stepped away from the others, hopped onto a counter, and plugged himself into a mystifying piece of equipment. Annabelle saw him fiddle with the screen on his belly. Then he unplugged himself and returned to the others. "Okay. I have a plan," he said. "Tomorrow night, as soon as Charlie and his crew have left the toy department, Viramax and I will tell the others what's really been happening—that you're in the doll hospital and there haven't been any kidnappings after all, so it will be safe to be loose in the store. Then we'll gather a group of dolls to come back to the hospital with us."

"You'd better make sure Marisol is one of them," said Mom Funcraft. "You're going to need someone tall."

"I hope she hasn't been sold," said Angelica.

"Fingers crossed," said Annabelle, feeling hopeful for the first time since Maggie had slammed her onto the counter.

"We'll have to take two escalators," said Vixamax.

"Four, really," said Annabelle. "Two up and two down."

"That's all right. Marisol can carry us."

"Won't the escalators be turned off by then?" asked Annabelle.

"Hmm," said Vixamax. "Maybe. If they

are, Marisol will walk up and down."

"I've just thought of another mess," said Mom with disapproval. "The hospital is locked at night. How will you get back in here?"

"I have the answer to that one," said Angelica. "I know where the spare key is kept. We'll slide it under the door when the rescue party arrives."

"And Marisol is tall enough to reach the lock," said Annabelle. "She can open the door."

"Ah. Nice and tidy," said Mom, looking relieved.

"We'll have you out of here in no time," added Vixamax. "And then we'll figure out how to get you guys home. All the way home, I mean . . . Angelica? What's the matter?"

"Her hand! Annabelle does need to have her hand fixed before she leaves here."

"That's right," said Annabelle. "I can't go back to the Palmers' with a broken hand any more than I can go back without my green hair."

"And what about Annabelle's work order?" said Angelica. "The person who's supposed to repair Annabelle on Monday will find a work order and no doll to go with it."

Everyone fell silent. At last Annabelle, a small smile on her lips, said, "I have an idea. It's a little risky, but I think it will work. We'll have to take a few chances."

"I like chances," said Vixamax.

"I don't," said Mom.

"We don't have a choice," said Annabelle. "Okay, listen. The only human who will be in here tomorrow is Miss Hollis, is that right?"

"Yes," said Vixamax. "Except for customers."

"Does anybody know where the blank work orders are kept?"

"Top drawer," said Angelica. "The one below the computer."

Annabelle nodded. "Then what about this idea? We'll get a blank work order and we'll fill it out for me, except that in the space where the repairs should be listed, the only thing we'll write is 'Glue cracks in hand.'"

"We'll leave the work order where Miss Hollis will be sure to see it," said Vixamax, "so she'll fix you tomorrow."

"And we'll have to get rid of the other work order," said Annabelle. She frowned. "Wait a second! What's going to happen on Monday when Mrs. Katz comes in and I'm not here?"

"Messy, messy," said Mom.

"Batter up!" said Viramax.

"Don't worry. Mrs. Katz won't be here again until Wednesday," said Vixamax. "And if she realizes you're gone, she'll just think you've been taken back downstairs already. She knows you're a store doll, like Viramax and me."

"Come on," said Angelica, pulling Annabelle to her feet. "Let's get started with the new work order right now."

"Who's going to do the writing?" asked Vixamax. "We need someone who can make big letters, like a human, and also copy Mrs. Katz's handwriting."

"I'll do it," said Annabelle. And she did. When she had finished, she placed the work order on top of the pile. Then she and Angelica tore the first one into tiny pieces, as small as if the paper had been shredded by a

McGinitie's
DOLL HOSPITAL
WORK ORDER

ITEM: *Doll with green hair*

arm

REPAIR BREAKDOWN

AUTHORIZATION:

mouse, and swept them over the edge of the counter and into a wastebasket below.

"Nice work," commented Mom.

"Anything else?" asked Annabelle.

Angelica shook her head.

"I don't think so," said Vixamax.

"Then," said Annabelle, "there's nothing to do but wait for tomorrow and hope that Miss Hollis repairs the twins and me."

"And that we can carry out the rescue operation tomorrow night," added Vixamax.

On Sunday afternoon, Miss Hollis showed up exactly when Vixamax had said she would. She repaired Annabelle first, then several other dolls, including Viramax. (She found no glitches in Vixamax.) When she closed up the hospital at the end of the afternoon, she took the twins with her, as she had been instructed to do.

Later, after Charlie and his crew had come and gone, Annabelle and Angelica sat side by side on their shelf, holding hands and waiting. The doll hospital had grown dark, except for the light coming through the windows, by the time Annabelle heard a scratching sound at the door. As planned, the biggest doll in the hospital (who was much bigger than Annabelle, but not nearly so big as Marisol) fetched the spare key from a hook beneath the counter and slid it under the door. Moments later, the door opened and in walked Marisol, the twins, and Tiffany.

"We're back!" announced Viramax, very pleased to have been repaired.

Annabelle and Tiffany shrieked when they saw each other, and Tiffany hugged Annabelle so fiercely that Annabelle feared her hand might break again.

"Come on, everybody," said Marisol. "We'd better get going."

Annabelle called good-bye to Mom Funcraft. She hugged Angelica and said, "If I don't see you again, I hope you find a new home very soon." Then, with one final glance over her shoulder at the lifeless Princess

Mimi, she followed her friends out the door.
Marisol locked it and slid the key back through
the crack. Moments later, Annabelle was on
her way to the second floor.

CHAPTER SIXTEEN

Mrs. Kay Robinson

ANNABELLE STEPPED around a rack of pajamas in Lingerie, then jumped backward as a small figure shot out from behind a lacy pink nightgown and shouted, "BOO!"

Annabelle let out a yelp.

"It's me! Matilda May!" said Tilly.

"Tilly!" Annabelle scooped her sister into her arms. "I missed you! . . . What are you doing here by yourself?"

"She's not by herself."

Bobby and Bailey emerged

from the pajamas and groaned as Annabelle approached them, arms open wide. "No hugging!" cried Bobby.

"Bobby took care of Tilly while you were away," said Tiffany.

"He is my good big brother," announced Tilly.

"Annabelle, we have great news," said Bobby. He glanced at Tiffany. "You didn't tell her yet, did you?"

"Tell me what?" asked Annabelle.

"Good. You kept the secret," said Bailey.

"What? What secret?" cried Annabelle.

"About Mrs. Kay Robinson," said Tilly importantly.

Annabelle looked confused. "The Palmers' neighbor?"

"Come on, you guys. Back to the toy department," said Marisol, striding through Lingerie and into Housewares on her long legs.

The smaller dolls ran after her, Bobby

holding Tilly by the hand, and presently Annabelle heard cheering and the thwack of a ball on a bat and knew that a game was in progress again.

As if she could read Annabelle's thoughts, Tiffany said, "Everything's pretty much back to normal here. Except that Dakota Jane was sold while you were in the hospital. Truck and all."

"Really?" said Annabelle. "I don't know whether to be happy or sad."

"Be happy," said Tiffany. "DJ is. Getting sold was her dream."

Annabelle nodded. Then she said, "So what is this big secret?"

"Let's go sit down," said Bobby, pointing to a quiet corner where a shelf of puzzles met a shelf of board games.

"One second," said Annabelle. She stood before the twins. "How can I ever thank you?"

"Don't hug us!" screeched Viramax, and he and his brother made a dash for the baseball game.

"How can I ever thank *you*?" Annabelle asked Marisol, and she threw her arms around Marisol's leg.

"No problem," said Marisol. She left to find Elsipad.

Annabelle sat on the floor with Tilly, Bobby, Bailey, and Tiffany. "Well?" she said.

"We made a great discovery while you were gone," said Tiffany.

"About Mrs. Kay Robinson," said Tilly.

"The Palmers' neighbor," agreed Annabelle. "But what does she have to do with anything?"

A long conspiratorial silence followed, during which Tiffany, Bailey, Bobby, and even Tilly May all looked smugly at Annabelle. Finally Bobby exclaimed, "She *works* here!"

"At McGinitie's," said Bailey.

"In Housewares," said Tiffany.

"Only part-time," said Bobby, "but she'll be here tomorrow."

"And one way or another," said Tiffany, "we're going to go home with her at the end of the day."

"By hook or by crook," said Tilly.

"But how?" asked Annabelle.

"We're going to climb into her bag—" Tiffany replied.

"She was carrying a tote bag," Bailey interrupted his sister.

"Into her *bag*," continued Tiffany, giving Bailey a pointed look, "and just ride home with her."

"We can't . . . I mean, how," sputtered Annabelle, "how are we going to do that without being seen?"

"We're not sure yet," said Tiffany. "But we've been gone for over a week, and we could be sold at any moment, so we *have* to get home. Now."

"I know, I know," said Annabelle. "But running through the store . . ."

"We did it on the day we got here and no one saw us," said Bailey. "Not until we were standing on a counter in full view."

"That's true," said Annabelle. "But getting from Mrs. Kay Robinson's house to the Palmers' . . ."

"Do you have a better idea?" asked Bobby.

"No," admitted Annabelle.

"We're going to make it work," said Tiffany.

And Annabelle, remembering when she had boldly written a new work order for herself and gotten rid of the old one, said, "Okay. Yes. We are going to make it work."

* * *

The plan was simple. Scary, but simple. In the morning, Marisol would not put Annabelle, Bobby, and Tilly back in the glass case as usual. And Tiffany and Bailey would not return to the play area. Instead, the five dolls would hide behind a stack of Monopoly boxes

on the bottom shelf of the board game display, which was just across the aisle from the china department in Housewares, where Tiffany was positive Mrs. Kay Robinson worked. "I heard her talking to Nell," Tiffany explained.

The dolls planned to watch for Mrs. Robinson when she arrived for work and to note were she put her tote bag. Then, at some quiet point during the day, they would make a run for the bag, climb inside, and hide—they hoped there would be something under which to hide. They also hoped Mrs. Robinson would go straight home after work.

"A plan with a lot of holes in it," said Annabelle, heaving a sigh.

"If it has holes in it, is it still a plan?" asked Bobby.

"Yes," said Tiffany. "Just not a very good one."

The next morning, Annabelle, Tiffany, Bailey, Bobby, and Tilly said good-bye to their friends and crept onto the shelf of games. And then they waited.

And waited.

And waited some more.

No Mrs. Kay Robinson.

Annabelle began to feel nervous. She kept her eye on Marcie, who so far had been too busy to peek into the glass display case. At eleven thirty, when the toy department and Housewares were bustling as, Annabelle supposed, was the rest of McGinitie's, Annabelle whispered to Tiffany, "Where's Mrs. Robinson? Shouldn't she be here by now?"

"I told you, she's part-time," said Tiffany. "She'll be here soon."

And she was. Promptly at noon, a woman carrying a Save Our Planet tote bag stepped off the elevator.

"There she is!" Bailey whispered loudly.

"She's carrying the bag. That's the first good thing," said Bobby.

"And now she's putting it on the floor, right where we hoped she would put it," said Tiffany. "That's the second good thing."

Annabelle was hoping for about a thousand more good things when she spied Marcie walking through the toy department.

"Hey!" Annabelle exclaimed softly. "Look, everybody."

Five pairs of doll eyes fastened themselves on Marcie. She was carrying Angelica back from the doll hospital.

"Angelica's smiling!" said Tiffany.

"I fink she's pretty," commented Tilly.

The dolls watched as Angelica was

returned to the glass case and placed on a stand, where she hung daintily, smiling down on the toy department.

The afternoon slipped away.

"What time does Mrs. Kay Robinson go home?" Tiffany whispered.

"When the store closes," Bobby replied.

"That's in an hour," said Bailey. "We don't have much time left."

"We still have to wait until not so many people are around," said Annabelle.

"If the plan doesn't work today, we could try it tomorrow," said Tiffany, sounding doubtful.

"No! Today! By hook or by crook," said Tilly May.

Annabelle slumped on the shelf. She was afraid of the journey ahead. But she agreed with Tilly, and she was feeling very impatient.

She stared around the toy department. She saw a boy in the play area building a house for a Funcraft family. She saw a woman looking at a baby doll who reminded Annabelle in a dizzying sort of way of her own Baby Betsy. And then she saw a girl and an older man standing in front of the glass case.

"Grandpa," said the girl, "that is the most beautiful doll ever." She was pointing to Angelica.

Annabelle grabbed Tiffany. "Tiff—"

But before she could finish her sentence, Bobby said in a loud whisper, *"Now!"* And

Bailey exclaimed, "Remember to hold hands!" Annabelle, clutching Bailey and Tilly May, found herself scrambling out of the hiding place.

If anyone in McGinitie's had been looking at just the right spot at that very moment, he would have seen five small dolls zip from the bottom shelf of a display in the toy department, run across the aisle and into Housewares, and crawl into a canvas bag lying on its side behind a checkout counter.

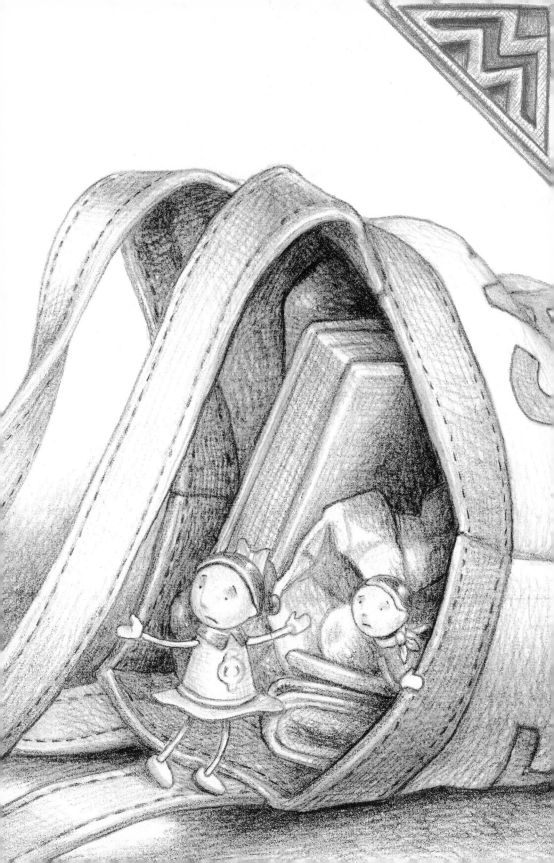

They were moving so fast that the last doll in the line, a particularly tiny girl, couldn't keep her feet on the floor and was being pulled along like a kite. But no human saw any of this happen. The dolls had chosen a moment of calm in which the few store customers were busy writing checks or examining price tags or talking to store clerks. Several dolls saw what happened, though, and silently wished their friends well.

And that was the last Annabelle, Bobby, Tilly, Bailey, or Tiffany saw of the toy department in McGinitie's.

They flung themselves well back in the bag and found plenty of things beneath which to hide. "Stay quiet," Annabelle cautioned Tilly.

Later, when the dolls heard the announcement that the store would be closing, Annabelle squeezed her eyes shut and, thinking of Elsipad, visualized a safe and uneventful trip home, which was exactly what followed.

"Good night, Kay," said a voice high above the dolls' heads.

"Good night," replied Mrs. Robinson. "See you tomorrow."

The bag was picked up in something of a hurry, it seemed to Annabelle, and carried through the store, down the escalator, and finally outside to the noises of the street. Several minutes later, Annabelle heard a car door open and felt the bag drop. She heard an engine start and thought, I'm riding in a car!

A few minutes later when the car slowed, turned a corner, and came to a stop, Annabelle tried to see Tiffany in the dark recesses of the bag, but she couldn't make out her face—and how she longed for a sign of encouragement from her friend. In this next moment, Mrs. Kay Robinson might simply scoop up the bag and take it inside her house before the dolls had a chance to escape. Or she might set it down outside the car.

"She *has* to set it down, she *must*," thought Annabelle desperately.

Mrs. Kay Robinson lifted the bag from the floor of the car and said, "Oh, I forgot to pick up the mail." Then she plopped the bag onto the driveway, where it again slumped on its side, and she walked away.

"Run!" said Bobby.

The dolls shot out of the bag and across the yard to the Palmers' lawn. They didn't stop until they had crossed it and were pushing their way through The Captain's door.

CHAPTER SEVENTEEN

Missing

WHEN THE LAST DOLL had
tumbled through The Captain's door and
landed inside, Annabelle held her finger to
her lips and signaled for quiet.

"What is it?" whispered Tiffany after a few moments had passed.

"I just want to make sure no one's around," Annabelle replied. "We've been gone a long time. What if Mrs. Robinson accidentally let The Captain out of the kitchen? Or even worse, what if one of the Palmers came back early while we were away?"

"That's not very likely," said Bobby.

"But it's possible," said Annabelle.

"There was no car in the driveway," said Bailey.

"But it could be in the garage, and the garage door was closed," Annabelle pointed out.

The dolls stood very still while the clock in the living room ticked away three long minutes.

At last Tiffany said, "I don't hear a single sound, Annabelle."

"All right. Let's go upstairs, then. But very quietly, just in case. As soon as we find our parents, we can make sure we're still really alone."

The dolls crept to the bottom of the staircase. As they climbed the steps, the older dolls taking turns pushing and pulling Tilly

May up each one, Annabelle realized that instead of the rush of happiness she had expected when she finally made her way home again, what she felt instead was that something was wrong. Very, very wrong.

At the top of the stairs, the dolls hurried through the hall. When they reached Kate's door, Annabelle, Bobby, and Tilly said good-bye to Tiffany and Bailey, who ran ahead to Nora's room.

"It's awfully quiet up here," Annabelle whispered to Bobby. "Something feels—"

"Wrong," Bobby finished for her. "I know."

Annabelle's steps grew leaden as they approached the stool below their house. Helping Tilly up any more stairs suddenly seemed impossible, so Annabelle stood on the floor, cupped her hands around her mouth, and called, "Mama? Papa?"

No answer. She and Bobby glanced at each other.

"Uncle Doll? Auntie Sarah?" called Bobby.

Nothing.

Annabelle tried raising her voice. "*Mama? Papa?*"

At last Nanny appeared timidly at the top of the steps. "Annabelle? Is that really you?"

"Yes!" cried Annabelle. "Bobby too. Um, and Tilly May." She hesitated. "What's the matter?"

Annabelle stepped back and saw that Baby Betsy and Tiffany's sister, Baby Britney, were seated on the floor behind Nanny.

"I'm very frightened," said Nanny in a voice so soft that Annabelle could barely hear her.

Annabelle saw Nanny's gaze shift to a spot across Kate's room, and she turned to see

Tiffany and Bailey come running through the door.

"No one's home at our house," announced Tiffany.

Annabelle glanced at Nanny. "Only Nanny and the babies are here."

"Everyone else is gone," whispered Nanny. "They left late last night to look for you—I stayed behind with Betsy and Britney—and I haven't seen them since. Oh, where *were* you? Where did you go?"

Annabelle and Tiffany made their way up the stool, leaving the boys on the floor with Tilly.

"We . . . we ran away," said Annabelle, giving Nanny a hug. "Because of Tilly. But we knew we'd made a mistake and we tried to come home, only we were stuck in a store and we couldn't find our way back. Oh, it's a long story. We'll tell you later. But what about Mama and Papa and the others?"

"They've gone out searching for you several times," Nanny answered, "and they've always come back after a few hours. Late last night they decided to try again. They promised to return this morning." Nanny spread her hands. "But I haven't heard a thing. I've been out calling, but it's hard because I have to leave the babies. I can't go far."

"We'll find them," Tiffany said confidently. "We promise."

Annabelle nodded. "Nanny, you stay here with Betsy and Britney. With Tilly too, if you don't mind."

The boys helped Tilly up the steps of the stool, and after more hugs with Nanny, the four dolls climbed back down and ran to Kate's door. Annabelle turned and waved to Nanny. She knew Nanny was afraid that this was the last she would see of Annabelle and Bobby and Tiffany and Bailey. Still, Nanny gave Annabelle a brave wave.

"What on earth could have happened?" asked Tiffany as the dolls hurried along the hallway.

"I don't know. We'd better just start searching," said Bobby. "Right here."

"And fast," added Bailey. "Let's split up. If anyone finds anything, shout for the others. Meet at the top of the stairs in twenty minutes."

The four dolls explored the rooms on the second floor. When twenty minutes had gone by, they met breathlessly at the top of the staircase.

"Nothing," said Annabelle.

"Nothing," said Tiffany and Bailey and Bobby.

"Downstairs then," said Annabelle, and she led the way. When they reached the bottom, she said, "Let's split up again. Tiffany, you take the dining room. Bobby and Bailey, you take the living room together, since it's big. I'll take the hallways and the mudroom. We'll meet back here in half an hour. Unless we find something."

Annabelle made a dash for the front
foyer. She checked behind an umbrella stand
and around the legs of a coatrack and under
a small chest of drawers where the Palmers
kept gloves and hats and odds and ends. It
was really too dark to see under the chest, so
Annabelle bravely swept her hands back and
forth as far as she could reach, and called,
"Hello?" and "Is anyone here?" But she
neither felt nor heard a thing.

She made a cursory check of the mudroom, thinking that if anything was amiss, she
would have noticed earlier when she had at
last pushed her way through The Captain's
door, which was nearby. So Annabelle
headed for the back hall. This short hallway
led from the mudroom toward the portion of
the house where The Captain was now resid-
ing. At one end was a door into the kitchen
(this was closed); at the other was the step
down to the mudroom. The hallway between,
not nearly as gritty and muddy as the actual
mudroom, was nevertheless messy. This was
where Kate and Nora dropped their backpacks and piles of books during the school
year, where shopping bags were set down,

where stray toys were tossed, and where anything landed when someone found it in the
house and didn't know where else to put it.

Annabelle peered behind bags and balls
and under abandoned backpacks. Nothing.
She noticed a jacket that had fallen from
its hook and she lifted it. Nothing.
And then she noticed the corner by
the kitchen door that was awash
in small toys. (Toy Soup, Mrs.
Palmer called this mess.)
Annabelle had been staring at
it for several seconds before
she realized that scattered
amid the pink ponies and
plastic purses and jacks and
jump ropes were Mama, Papa,
Mom Funcraft, Dad Funcraft,
Auntie Sarah, and Uncle Doll. They
lay at all angles and in all positions,
and looked as stiff and as lifeless as Mean
Mimi had looked when she had lain in
Kate's room so many months ago.

Annabelle let out a cry, a long wail
that ended in a sob. "Bobby!" she called.
"Bobby! Tiffany! Bailey! Come here *quick*!"

They didn't arrive immediately, so Annabelle ran through the hall and was about to scramble down the step into the mudroom, when she saw the others. "Here! Come here!" she yelped. "Wait until you see."

Moments later, Annabelle, Bobby, Bailey, and Tiffany stood looking down at the Toy Soup. No one spoke. Finally Bailey stepped forward and poked his father with his foot. Then he leaned over and touched his mother's back. He glanced at Tiffany.

"Doll State for sure," murmured Tiffany. "Maybe even Per—"

"Don't say it!" exclaimed Annabelle.

"I wonder what *happened*?" said Bobby. "How could they all end up like this? All six of them at the same time?"

"I don't know," said Annabelle, voice

quavering, "but we're responsible for it. They were out searching for *us*."

"But no one else is here," said Tiffany. "No humans, I mean. So who saw them?"

"Does anything else cause Doll State?" asked Annabelle.

No one knew.

"I wonder when they'll wake up," said Bailey.

Tiffany shook her head. Then she said, "Two of us should go back upstairs and tell Nanny what we found. And stay with her. She looks like she needs company. The others should stay here."

In the end, the dolls decided that the boys would return to Nanny, and that Annabelle and Tiffany would keep watch over their parents and Auntie Sarah and Uncle Doll.

All that night, Annabelle and Tiffany sat on the floor in the hallway, listening to the nighttime sounds, talking occasionally, but mostly just waiting. Annabelle heard the clock in the living room chime the hours, and remembered guarding the toy department in McGinitie's and calling out "All's well." At long last she heard the clock chime five, then six, and then seven. Fifteen minutes later, the little dolls in the Toy Soup stirred and sat up.

"Mama!" cried Annabelle. "Papa! You're alive!"

And suddenly everyone was talking and exclaiming, the grown-ups sounding sleepy.

"What happened?" Tiffany asked desperately. "Were you in Doll State?" (She decided she would never let the grown-ups forget this.)

"What happened to *you*?" said Papa Doll. "What day is this? Do you know how long we've been searching for you?"

"We've been trying to get back," said Annabelle. "The boys too. But we couldn't. Not until yesterday." She tried to explain what had happened.

"Well, you're back now, and we're all okay," said Auntie Sarah practically, and with that, everyone stood and began hugging.

"Uh-oh," said Uncle Doll suddenly. "What time is it? What *time* is it?"

"About twenty after seven," replied Annabelle.

"Everybody upstairs. Pronto," said Uncle Doll.

"But—" Tiffany began to say.

"No buts. Come on." Uncle Doll led the way to the stairs.

As the eight dolls puffed and gasped and pulled and climbed, Dad Funcraft said, "In case you kids are wondering, we went out searching for you two nights ago." (Annabelle detected a note of resentment in his voice.) "And yesterday morning Mrs. Robinson showed up much earlier than usual to give The Captain his breakfast. She ran into us on her way to the kitchen. I don't know what she saw—"

"Or thinks she saw," said Auntie Sarah.

"—but we found ourselves in Doll State immediately."

"We certainly don't want to run into her

again," added Mom Funcraft. "Which is why we'd better get home right away."

The dolls reached the top step and ran toward Kate's room.

"Mama," said Annabelle, "Papa, there's something I have to tell you. We have Tilly May with us."

"We thought you might," replied Papa.

CHAPTER EIGHTEEN

What Will Become of Tilly May?

LONG BEFORE the dolls had finished making their way up the steps to Annabelle's house, Nanny appeared above them and exclaimed, "You're back! Oh, you're back!"

Bobby and Bailey clattered through the Dolls' parlor. "What happened?" they cried.

"Doll State," said Annabelle.

"Mrs. Robinson saw them," said Tiffany.

"I am so embarrassed," said Uncle Doll.

"Oh, for corn's sake," said Auntie Sarah.

The talking stopped when Tilly May appeared next to Nanny. "Annabelle!" she called.

"Hi, Tilly," said Annabelle.

For the next few moments no one said a word. Annabelle and Tiffany scrambled up the top step and ran inside the house. Then Annabelle turned and waited for the adults to finish the climb. This was accomplished with much gasping and groaning, and Uncle Doll said, "I'm not as young as I used to be," which made no sense at all, since he was exactly the same age he had always been.

When at last the dolls, all fourteen of them, were crowded into the house, Mama and Papa stood looking at Tilly May, and then Mama stooped and took Tilly's hands in her own. Annabelle wanted to say, "Do you see, Mama? Do you see that Tilly must be part of our family?" But instead she stepped back and put her arm around Auntie Sarah's waist.

"My goodness," whispered Mama. She glanced at Papa, and finally Papa knelt down too.

"Well," he said. "Well."

"She's the spitting image of Annabelle," spoke up Auntie Sarah.

Tilly looked at the faces of Annabelle's parents. She studied them for a long time. At last she said, "Are you my mama and papa?"

"Yes," said Mama. "I believe we are."

Annabelle wasn't surprised to find that what followed was more hugging. So much hugging, in fact, that Bobby and Bailey left the room, Bobby calling over his shoulder, "Tell us when the disgusting part is over."

The disgusting part included more hugging (of course) and some crying. And when it was finally over—when Mama had wiped her tears on the hem of her sleeve, and Papa had cleared his throat and patted his cheeks with a handkerchief—Nanny took Tilly, Betsy, and Britney upstairs to the nursery. It was then that Dad Funcraft eyed Annabelle, Bobby, Bailey, and Tiffany and said, "Now it's time to talk."

"Uh-oh," said Tiffany.

"Into the parlor," said Papa.

Everyone sat down, the adults on chairs and the sofa, the children on the floor, and Mom Funcraft said, "Do you kids have any idea what you did by running away?"

Annabelle squirmed. "Yes. We have an

idea now. But in the beginning we just wanted to save Tilly, and we didn't know what else to do. We had already tried talking to you," she added, looking at her parents.

"But Annabelle, for heaven's sake," said Mama. "What was running away going to accomplish?"

Annabelle shrugged uncomfortably.

"Nothing. We realized it on the very first day," spoke up Tiffany. "But by the time we decided to come home, we were already lost in the woods."

"The woods!" exclaimed Uncle Doll.

"We have a lot to tell you," Tiffany said.

"Do you know how frightened we were?" asked Mom Funcraft. "We had no idea what had happened to you. Our *children*. We didn't know if we'd ever see you again. And without our children, well . . ."

Annabelle let her head drop.

"Something else," said Dad, "and I want to make this very clear. If the four of you had not come home by the time the Palmers returned, we"—here Dad Funcraft waved his hand to indicate that all the adults in the room agreed with him—"believe the situation might have put dollkind in jeopardy. And what the result of that would have been, we don't know."

"But it would have been serious," said Uncle Doll. "Very serious."

"Are we going to be punished?" asked Bobby.

"There will be consequences," replied Papa.

"It was scary seeing you in Doll State," said Bailey in a small voice.

"Yes, we know," replied Auntie Sarah. "And we realize you knew early on that you had made a mistake."

"And were trying to fix it," added Mama.

"Still . . ." said Mom Funcraft.

"There will be consequences," repeated Papa.

Mama nodded. "But we'll talk about those later. Right now we have a more immediate problem."

"What to do about Tilly?" guessed Annabelle.

"Exactly," said Auntie Sarah.

"Tilly can't just appear in our house," said Papa.

Uncle Doll shook his head. "Especially not if the Palmers open the package down-stairs and find it empty."

"Well, couldn't we hide her?" asked Annabelle desperately.

"Forever?" said Mama. "I don't think so. Eventually she would be found. And then too many questions would be raised. Especially since she looks so much like you, Annabelle. Someone would be bound to remember the empty package."

"But, but—" Annabelle jumped to her feet. "What if we put Tilly May in the package and the Palmers send it back? We can't do that to Tilly. We're her family!"

"Hey," said Tiffany, "I just thought of something. Annabelle, Grandma Katherine hasn't seen the package yet, remember?"

"Yes," said Annabelle, sending a fierce scowl in the direction of her parents.

"When she does, don't you think she'll recognize the name on the label, just like you did? She'll realize it's her grandfather's name, and of course she'll want to open the box."

"But what if she doesn't recognize the name?" said Annabelle.

"What if she does?" countered Auntie Sarah.

"What if—" Annabelle began.

"Ahem. Couldn't someone say, 'Good thinking, Tiffany'?" said Tiffany grumpily.

"Good thinking, Tiffany," said Bobby. "I mean, that really was good thinking. Because

I have a feeling that what you said is exactly what is going to happen."

"So do I," said Auntie Sarah.

Papa looked across Kate's room at the calendar hanging over her desk. "When are the Palmers coming back?" he asked. "We need to make a plan."

"Saturday," said Annabelle.

"Grandma Katherine might be coming back on Friday, though," said Mom Funcraft.

"But no one will be coming home before Friday?"

Mom shook her head. "I don't think so."

"Well then," said Papa, "sometime early on Friday morning we'll have to put Tilly back in the package. We'll make sure to seal it up so it looks just as it did when the Palmers left, and we must leave it in the exact spot on the couch in which the Palmers last saw it." Papa paused. "And then . . . and then we'll have to leave Tilly and return to our places and hope that things happen the way Tiffany suggested they will."

Annabelle let out a groan. "Suppose no one comes home until Saturday night? Oh, I can't bear to think of Tilly May back in that little dark prison. All alone . . . Could we at least sit outside the box and talk to her and maybe sing songs? She likes some singer named Rosemary Clooney."

"And risk the Palmers returning and finding you downstairs?" said Mama. "Absolutely not. Tilly goes back into the package on Friday, and we resume our lives up here."

"And hope for the best," said Mom Funcraft.

And that is what the dolls did. But first they made the most of the three days that remained before the Palmers' vacations came to an end.

"Three days," said Annabelle crabbily to Tiffany. "*Three days.* We were supposed to have *fourteen* days of freedom. And we wasted them by running away."

It was a testament to their best friendship that Tiffany refrained from saying, "And whose idea was it to run away?" Instead she said, "Well, at least our punishment isn't going to start until after the Palmers are back." (Once the Palmers had returned, Annabelle and Bobby were not to be allowed to play with Tiffany and Bailey for an entire month, nor even to leave the house unless Kate took them out. And Papa had hinted at other consequences.) "So let's not waste any more days. What do you want to do, Annabelle?"

Annabelle drew up a list. This is the list:

1. Show the grown-ups how to play baseball

2. See what's in Kate's desk

3. Find the remote and show Tilly May what's on TV

4. Turn on Kate's computer and check out the American iDoll Web site

5. Have a birthday party for Tilly even though we don't know when her birthday is

6. Make up fake boyfriends

7. See if we're big enough to move the Monopoly pieces

8. If yes, play Monopoly

Annabelle and Tiffany crossed each item off the list as soon as it was accomplished. (They named their fake boyfriends Charles and Vixamax. "But Vixamax doesn't have anything to do with the real Vixamax," said Tiffany. "I don't want *him* for my boyfriend. I just like his name.") On Thursday night, Mama Doll finally got to give her party. It was a huge success.

Before Annabelle knew it, Friday morning had arrived.

"Do you remember what's going to happen to you today?" Mama asked Tilly as sunshine crept into Kate's room.

Tilly was sitting on the floor playing with Baby Betsy. "I have to go back in the box fing?" she said.

"That's right. And do you understand why?"

"So the old lady can find me and take me out?"

"And you can live here forever with us," said Annabelle.

No one had told Tilly that there was a teensy chance the box might be mailed back to London.

"Okay," said Tilly.

Mama, Papa, Auntie Sarah, Uncle Doll, Annabelle, and Bobby accompanied Tilly downstairs and helped her onto the couch. Annabelle opened the package.

"You won't be in the box for long," said Mama. "We'll see you very soon."

"Okay," said Tilly.

The Dolls kissed Tilly May, and she crawled through the dark opening. Annabelle resealed the tape.

"Good-bye! Good-bye, Tilly!" called the Dolls.

"I love you!" added Annabelle.

"I love you too," said Tilly.

The Dolls made their way to the edge of the couch.

From inside the box, they heard a small voice sing, "Ain't a-gonna need this house no longer, ain't a-gonna need this house no more."

Wilson and Sons
1 Scala Street
London, England

William Seaborn Cox esq
26 Wetherby Lane
Reade, Connecticut
America

BY AIR MAIL
par avion
Royal Mail

"Tilly," said Papa, "you have to keep very still now. No more talking or singing, remember? The Palmers could come back at any moment."

"Okay," said Tilly, and she fell silent.

The Dolls returned to their house. The Funcrafts settled themselves in Nora's room.

Early that evening, Grandma Katherine came home.

The next afternoon, the rest of the Palmers came home.

Annabelle, who Kate had left seated tidily in the parlor of the Dolls' house, heard the arrivals, heard doors opening and closing, heard shouts and exclamations. But from her perch in Kate's room she had no idea what had happened to the little package on the couch in the living room.

CHAPTER NINETEEN

A Home for Tilly May

FTER THE PALMERS returned on Saturday, Annabelle expected Tilly's arrival at the Dolls' house to take place at any moment. She was sure that every step on the stairs was Grandma Katherine bearing Tilly May, every voice in the hallway was Kate exclaiming over her new doll. But dinnertime came and went, and then Kate's bedtime came and went, and no Tilly.

Late that night, when the Palmers' household was quiet and no one was awake except dolls, Annabelle left her place in the parlor and found her parents in the kitchen.

"What do you suppose has happened?" she asked tremulously.

Mama and Papa shook their heads, and Annabelle could tell they were as worried as she.

"Maybe the Palmers haven't opened the package yet," said Bobby, leaning against the icebox.

"Maybe they haven't opened it because they don't think it's for them," said Annabelle. "Maybe Grandma Katherine hasn't even seen it. Kate's father might already have stuck it somewhere, ready to take to the post office on Monday."

"Oh, Annabelle, a thousand things could have happened," said Mama. "It doesn't do any good to speculate."

But Annabelle didn't know what else she could do. She and Tiffany were no longer allowed to visit. And since there was very little moonlight to see by, Annabelle was stuck in the dark, waiting and stewing and picturing Tilly May sealed into her box.

The next morning, Kate rose early. She left her room before breakfast and didn't return until after lunch. When she did, she was followed by Nora and Grandma Katherine. Grandma Katherine was holding something carefully in her cupped palms.

"It's awfully hard to believe," she was saying.

"But we always wondered about Baby Betsy, didn't we?" said Kate. "I mean, why was she sent as the Dolls' baby? She's so much bigger than they are."

"There are such things as giants, you know," said Nora.

"But most baby giants aren't as big as their parents,

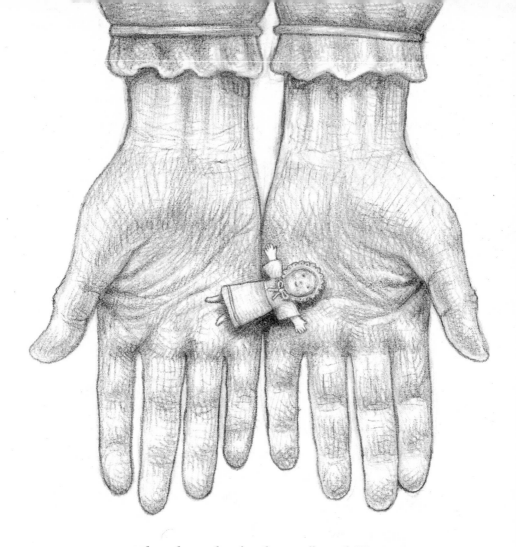

not right when they're born," said Kate.

"Well, anyway," said Grandma Katherine, "this is almost a miracle. Imagine, the great-grandson of the original doll maker finding this package after so many years—a century. We're lucky he decided to mail it, and we're lucky our family still lives in this house."

"The first doll maker must have realized

his mistake," said Kate, "and he tried to send this dolly to your grandfather way back when it was still the eighteen hundreds."

"What was the name of the man who sent the package?" asked Nora.

"Geoffrey Watson," replied Grandma Katherine.

"Is Mr. Watson a doll maker too?"

"The letter didn't say. Just that he was remodeling the shop—the old doll maker's shop, I suppose—and he found the package behind a cabinet. He said he guessed it had fallen there."

"And no one found it," said Kate dreamily, "for over one hundred years. Just think, this little girl doll could have lived here with the Dolls all that time."

"She looks like Annabelle," spoke up Nora.

"She does indeed," agreed Grandma Katherine.

Kate stood before her dollhouse and said, "Ahem. I have an announcement to make. Dolls, your long-lost little sister is here."

Kate took Tilly May from Grandma

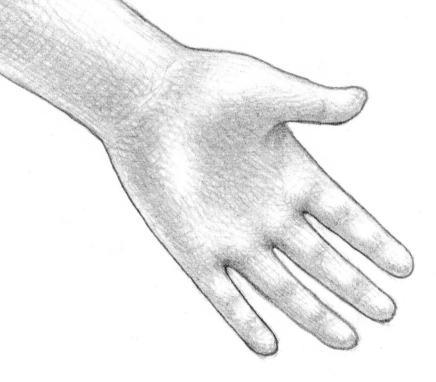

Katherine. "See?" she said. "This is your new home. Hey, I wonder where's she's going to sleep."

Annabelle thought, She can share my bed.

"We'll have to get another bed," said Grandma Katherine. "Maybe tomorrow we can go to the dollhouse store."

"Oh, yes! Please!" cried Kate and Nora.

And Nora added, "Can we *each* get some–

thing for our houses? Please, please, please?"

"I think we can do that," said Grandma Katherine.

Kate reached into the house and gathered the Doll family in the parlor. She posed Mama and Papa on the sofa, and then she set Tilly May between them. "Here is your new daughter," she said grandly.

"Your new *old* daughter, you mean," said Nora.

"Whatever," said Kate.

Grandma Katherine and Nora left Kate's room, but Kate remained in front of the Dolls' house, studying the little family. At last she too started to leave, but then she turned around, regarded the Dolls again, and said, "Huh," before crossing her room. At the doorway, she paused and looked once more at the dollhouse. "I wonder," she said, and at last she left her room.

Annabelle didn't dare move, but her heart was singing, and she risked a small smile at Tilly.

That night, as soon as Papa called softly, "The coast is clear!" the Dolls made a big fuss over Tilly May. Annabelle jumped up and down, and Bobby said, "High five!" and all the grown-ups hugged Tilly until she said, "I'm being squozen."

"You're home for good!" exclaimed Annabelle.

"Just what Tiffany said would happen," said Bobby.

"But even better because there seems to have been a letter in the package," said Auntie Sarah. "So now we know more of the story."

"Where was the letter?" Annabelle asked Tilly.

"All folded up," she replied. "In a corner."

"And no one suspected anything when they opened the box?" asked Uncle Doll.

"Grandma Kaferine said, 'My stars, this tape certainly isn't very sticky.' That's all."

The Dolls breathed sighs of relief.

"Our family is getting pretty big," observed Bobby. "The nursery is going to be crowded after Kate buys the new bed."

"Still, there's room for all of us," said Mama.

"Room for two babies?" asked Annabelle.

"They're both part of our family. We're all where we belong now. Tilly May is a Doll and so is Baby Betsy, and they will be ours forever and ever, and we will be theirs."

And that is how Tilly May Doll found her family and her home.

THE